# The Doctor's House
## and Other Fiction

Cary Fagan

Stoddart

*To my mother and father*

Published in 2000 by Stoddart Publishing Co. Limited
34 Lesmill Road, Toronto, Canada M3B 2T6
180 Varick Street, 9th Floor, New York, NY 10014

Distributed in Canada by General Distribution Services Ltd.
325 Humber College Blvd., Toronto, Canada M9W 7C3
Tel. (416) 213-1919   Fax (416) 213-1917
Email cservice@genpub.com

For information about U.S. publication and
distribution of Stoddart Books, contact
180 Varick Street, 9th Floor, New York, NY 10014

04   03   02   01   00      1   2   3   4   5

**Canadian Cataloguing in Publication Data**

Fagan, Cary
The doctor's house and other fiction

ISBN 0-7737-6107-1

I. Title.
PS8561.A375D6   2000      C813'.54      C99-933123-X
PR9199.3.F33D6   2000

"The Doctor's House" originally appeared in 1996
in a book of that title, published by paperplates books.

The other stories appearing here were first published in 1990
in a book entitled *History Lessons: Stories and Novellas*,
published by Hounslow Press.

Cover Photograph: K. Schermerhorn/Photonica
Cover Design: Angel Guerra
Text Design: Tannice Goddard

THE CANADA COUNCIL | LE CONSEIL DES ARTS
FOR THE ARTS | DU CANADA
SINCE 1957 | DEPUIS 1957

*We acknowledge for their financial support of our
publishing program the Canada Council, the Ontario Arts
Council, and the Government of Canada through the
Book Publishing Industry Development Program (BPIDP).*

Printed and bound in Canada

# Contents

# Nora
# by the Sea

$\mathcal{F}$rom the window Nora watched the car, a mustard Citroën, jerking out of the hotel drive as if it were in one of those Mack Sennett comedies they had once laughed over. The Citroën paused where the drive met the road, beyond which rose a tangled wall of subtropical trees and, farther, the tiled roofs of private estates. Directly below, when Nora leaned against the window, she could see new guests tumbling out of a taxi and the hotel porter starting to unload their baggage.

When she looked again the Citroën had disappeared. And with it her husband, Michael, who only yesterday had learned how to drive a standard shift when Nora had endured the ninety minutes down to Cannes. Not again; Michael would have to go without her, and besides, she looked forward to being alone — if keeping an eye on four children and a seventy-two-year-old man could be called being alone. This morning for the first time she had put on the yellow dress purchased in Paris, sandals on her feet, and silver earrings like seashells made by one of her own craftspeople. She felt light and summery; perhaps for once she even fit her name, Nora, like one of those cheerful English girls in wartime films that Michael used to tease she'd been named after.

She turned from the window and walked — waddled, the children exaggerated when they wanted to be mean — through the bedroom and across the hallway to the facing room whose door was unlocked. Her children's room was, as expected, a disaster, the three beds and extra cot like separate war zones, yesterday's underwear strewn about, and the wrappers from the chocolates left each morning on the pillows heaped on top of the television set which had been left on to a bicycle race. Nora turned off the television and picked up the underwear, not because she had failed in resisting the inheritance of her own mother's fastidiousness (at home her kids could make as much mess as they cared to live in), but out of respect for the maid. Then she stepped onto the balcony.

How odd that this hotel, with its air of archaic charm, should actually be quite modern, having been built in the early seventies in the international style that, according to the better magazines, was now discredited. Perhaps it was the way the hotel nestled into the cliff, its series of levels connected by stairs and escalators. Nora stood against the aluminum rail and felt her dress flutter against her legs. The sea was turquoise and dotted with boats. She could hear gulls. All of it — the view, the softness of the air — gave her a feeling of both stillness and movement. Just as she had wanted; just as she had hoped.

This stretch of shore, far below the hotel, was all rock and cliff, too dangerous for swimming. To the children's disappointment there wasn't a decent beach for twenty miles but Nora was glad of the isolation and the touch of wildness. From here down to the water there was no path, just glinting rock and scrub and, on either side of the hotel property, more estates with flat rectangles behind them that were tennis courts. The hotel pool two levels below was, at this time of morning, deserted. Nora could also see the informal garden, canopied with palm leaves, the stone steps that ran down to the pool, and the hotel's outdoor café with its round tables and wicker chairs. She also saw, sitting at one of those tables, her elder son.

Ananda, she could see, was writing in the journal she had given him before the trip. Her purpose had been to focus his attention on a family holiday he had resisted joining and to improve his writing skills, for his grades were poor. But she never could have predicted that Ananda would hardly put the journal down since the trip's beginning and that he would be there now, scribbling away, with a demitasse cup and a croissant set before him.

She was, of course, pleased about the journal, if not with the sight of a fifteen-year-old drinking espresso. That was too much, even if the management was French. She couldn't forbid Ananda, that wasn't how the family operated, but she could open a little reasoned discussion on the effects of caffeine. Nora, about to turn away, paused: from inside the hotel the waitress had appeared. She wore the typical black dress complete with frilly apron that showed a lot of stockinged leg and Nora recognized her as the same young woman who, dressed in grey and with a kerchief holding back her hair, came in to make their beds. Apparently the staff, despite the hotel's size, did double duty, like a family-run pension. The waitress had a rather sweet round face and a good figure and Ananda, who had refused to look happy for days, smiled.

Nora was again about to turn away when a man appeared, sweeping the café floor with a twig broom. He was another who did double service, for she recognized the same young athletic fellow who acted as porter. This was becoming a little drama; the waitress said something to the athletic man and then disappeared into the hotel. The athletic man leaned on the broom, next to Ananda but without speaking as Ananda, to his mother's amazement, tore a page from his journal, folded it, and placed it in the athletic man's back pocket. The man, carrying the broom, disappeared by the same door as the waitress.

That her own chronically shy Ananda had the courage to send a note to the waitress deserved his mother's admiration, accompanied by a perceptible tightening of anxiety. Certainly he deserved a relief from the months of moody silence, the evenings alone in his bedroom engaged in what seemed hours of desperate masturbation. Nora would not interfere now except to watch and, if she could, prevent her son from being hurt. No, not even that; this was her son's experience, not hers. She felt her heart beating, as if a car had brushed her. Yet a moment later she was already pleased with her decision. What a good day it would finally be, she was sure of that now.

A blueprint of the hotel's complex series of levels, its multiple staircases and escalators, would have appeared as confusing as a labyrinth, but the orienting views of sea or road from the high windows allowed guests (Nora had gone in search of her other children) to know just where they were. The colours of the hotel's interior were desert — white, grey, beige, yellow — the windows like lush paintings on the walls. For a hotel this size the halls seemed quiet to Nora, perhaps the result of a lower occupancy than the developers had anticipated, owing to the distance from Cannes. But this morning she liked feeling that any moment might bring an unexpected meeting round a corner and, indeed, she had two on her way down to the first level. The first was with the widow from Switzerland who yesterday had confided to Nora that she had not taken a holiday since the death of her husband. The second was not really a surprise for she heard the party of Germans before she saw them yawning their way into the dining room. Nora took the next door outside — there seemed to be dozens leading to the paths around the grounds — and breathed in the fecund air that sent a run of shocks along her thin allergic nose.

Nora started and looked down; the hotel's sleek tom was rubbing against her legs. She believed that cats (not dogs, including their own Lhasa apso — they liked everybody) were innate judges of character and as she bent down to scratch this one's gingery ears she was happy to take its appearance as another omen for the day. And looking ahead she saw, just before the gravel path disappeared round a corner, the twins.

Nora never said "the twins" aloud and had always insisted on their being treated as individuals; but as even now, at the age of eleven, they spent all their time together, it seemed natural to think of them as a pair, not the same but complementary. "What's up?" she said coming towards them. Gordon gave his infamous grin. Eileen giggled.

"Look, Mom," Gordon said, getting up to drag her over by the hand. He still wore the cabbie's cap that he had insisted on buying from a street vendor in London, his hair tucked inside and the brim turned up. With his wide face, big eyes and tremendous smile he looked — goofy.

"I almost caught a lizard. We've been trying all morning. But he got away, see?"

On the ground a lizard's tail. Writhing.

"Do you think it hurt when the tail came off?" Eileen said, her face a frown of concern. She had a sprinkling of freckles across her nose that could be accounted for in the family even if the fragile blondish-red hair couldn't.

"No, he didn't even feel it, did he, Mom? The tail just grows back."

"I don't suppose he enjoyed it much. Gordon, why do you wear your hat like that?" she said, fixing it. But he pushed her away and tipped up the brim again. Gordon liked to look goofy.

"Did you two have breakfast?"

"Uh-huh," Eileen said and began a careful explanation of how the four languages on the cereal box required different amounts of space.

"Can we go swimming?" Gordon asked.

"A little later. Where's Rose?"

"Outside Grandpa's door, waiting for him to wake up. Boy, does he ever sleep late."

"Mom," Eileen said and as she hesitated Nora could tell she was working out her thoughts. One needed a good deal of patience to have a conversation with Eileen. "Why do different languages take different room? I mean, aren't they just different words for the same thing?"

"I don't think so," Nora said — had she made a mistake not enrolling Eileen in French immersion? — "Languages aren't like pairs of shoes all the same. They're — let's see, now — like shoes of different colours and when you put them on you dance in a whole different way."

"Oh," was all she said, but she was thinking.

"Can we go swimming?"

"I said later, Gordon. Right now I'm going to have some breakfast with Ananda. Where are you two going to be?"

Gordon squinted up at her.

"That's classified information."

Eileen giggled.

The path that Nora continued on wound past the kitchen window that opened on hinges like elbows and from which drifted the same Madonna tune the kids were listening to on their Walkman these days. The café was entered through a trellis of vines in blossom beneath which Nora stood for a moment, the sound of a bee near her ear, looking at her son. The half-eaten croissant forgotten, he was absorbed in writing, his left hand clutching the pen near its nib and his face inches from the page. He wore army shorts picked up at some secondhand shop back in Toronto and a T-shirt imprinted with a grainy portrait of some new-wave band, just bought in London. How Nora loathed that haircut of his, shorter than a marine's, his scalp visible in spots and a little tuft at the back. Why couldn't he see that the haircut violated his beautiful and gentle face? Besides, the vaguest sense of history ought to have told him what such a military look signified to her generation; his own father had come to Canada to avoid the war, a story he had heard for years. Why, he looked just like the students they had once called — she could hardly say it, even to herself — fascists.

But fascists didn't wear earrings, at least not in her day, two bronze studs in a single lobe. These Nora liked, almost.

"Ananda," she said, but too quietly for him to hear. She loved his name that was so like a poem and that she and Michael had carried back with them from India where they had lived for eight months after her graduation. Of course she had returned to Toronto and the competence of Mount Sinai Hospital for the birth, but the name — meaning "joy" and in India as common as "Frank" — still meant for her that state of grace in which she and Michael had lived. As for Ananda himself, its vague femininity and foreignness would have been embarrassments enough, but as he grew older his name became a reminder of the appalling fact of his own conception. When he came home at the start of every school year, complaining, she and Michael would give the same response: "It's nice to be a little different." "No it isn't," Ananda would grumble. He still hadn't forgiven them.

It was seeing Ananda so withdrawn into the privacy of his journal that caused the first uneasiness of the day, that it could be something other than lovely. But she refused to let his slapping shut of the journal or the suppressed little frown as he looked up wound her. "Good morning," she kissed his cheek while he slipped his pen into a pocket on his shorts, meant for a bayonet or something worse. The speech on caffeine could wait for another time. Besides, how could *she* talk, who with Michael and two of his college friends had once dropped acid while hiking up Mount Rainier in Washington?

"Don't you want to finish your breakfast?"

"I've had enough," he said. "Where's Dad?"

"Gone to Cannes. He won't be home until this evening. I've got an idea, Since you're so interested in films, why don't you go in with him tomorrow? You can see a film at the festival, maybe even attend one of the press conferences and see a director."

"I don't think so, I'd rather just stay here. We're leaving the day after tomorrow, aren't we?"

"That's right. We fly to Paris and then home."

"You aren't going to change the ticket and make us stay longer?"

"Has it been so horrible to be with us?"

"I didn't mean it that way."

"I know, that's not what I meant to say either. I think it's been our best holiday in a long time."

"Sure." He pushed his chair back and rose.

"Where are you going?" There was, against her will, the slightest note of panic in her voice. "Won't you keep me company?"

"I want to go for a walk."

"Where?"

"Just around."

He walked away with that springy gait of his, bouncing on the balls of his feet. Nora watched him cross the café and hesitate before the trellis, not because he was reconsidering, as Nora momentarily hoped, but because the waitress was coming through from the other side. She smiled at him — it seemed to Nora conspiratorial — as he let her pass.

But Nora would not let herself brood over Ananda, nor over the failures of the holiday, for the weather was too fine and she could not think of a prettier place to sit than at this café table. She had looked forward to a day alone but now she wished that Michael was here and that they could have the kind of talk that had once been so frequent and expected between them. When she and Michael had met she was the only Canadian student at the small Massachusetts college and he was a teaching assistant from New Jersey who made experimental films. One of his films had won an award at a state film festival and he was trying to raise money for a more ambitious project which already had the name *Quantum*. He wore his hair in a pony tail and was prepared to leave the country to avoid the draft.

They did leave after Nora graduated, using the money he had raised to take them to Europe, the Middle East, India. On returning to Toronto they had moved into a cooperative house and Nora, waiting for the birth of their child, began to make jewellery, imitating the designs she had studied in her fine arts courses and had sketched in India. Michael started hunting for more money to make *Quantum* and took a job as assistant manager of an art cinema. Eight months later he was working for the country's largest movie-house chain, soothing his conscience with calculations of the money he could save. The job meant cutting off his pony tail. He began wearing ties.

Michael got promoted and *Quantum* never got made. At present he was vice-president in charge of Ontario distribution, had developed an obsessive interest in espionage films, and wore his hair, if not in a pony tail, at least elegantly long. They had renovated their third house, in Moore Park. Nora, between bearing children, had gone from selling her own work to hiring other jewellery makers and opening miniature boutiques in department stores. She now had twenty-one craftspeople, eleven stores, and her designs had just been featured in *Toronto Life*.

The trip to Cannes had been something of a perk for Michael, who was only peripherally involved in choosing films for distribution. But he was spending a few days attending screenings and lunching with producers, getting, as he told Nora, a larger sense of the business. Yesterday she had accompanied him to Cannes only to endure frantic crowds, soundtracks blaring from speakers, traffic jams caused by Finnish and Israeli television crews. In a hotel lobby a young woman, hoping to be discovered by a Hollywood director, had dropped her robe for the newspaper photographers. Nora and Michael had entered the hushed ambience of the hotel restaurant whose prices had been doubled for the festival and where Michael received the supplications of an independent film maker from New York. She was surprised to see her husband, author of the never-made *Quantum*, play with him so ruthlessly.

Nora wanted some coffee but lacked the courage to attract the waitress's attention and merely pulled apart the end of Ananda's croissant, leaving a buttery gleam on her fingers. The waitress appeared just outside the trellis but turned her back as Nora waved; the gentleman at the next table raised a sympathetic eyebrow and returned to his Italian newspaper. Three weeks ago Nora had sat on the living room sofa, holding the small brass Krishna that usually stood on the mantle next to the menorah, and waited for Michael to come home. She had heard the sound of his Mazda pulling into the drive and watched him come through the door, briefcase and squash racquet under his arm as he juggled with his keys.

"Michael," she had said. "I'm not happy."

Michael had stood there, his smile frozen, looking so much like Gordon, a clumsy enthusiastic boy. He put the racquet on an armchair.

"What we need is a little vacation," he had said, still smiling. It's been years since we've gone to Europe. How about it?"

Nora had looked down at the Krishna, waving its arms and legs. "All right," she had said. And then as an afterthought, "If we can bring the kids. And my father."

Six days in London, six days in Paris, and now the Riviera. They had waited hours to get into the Tower and the Louvre, had been swindled by no fewer than three taxi drivers, while the children, spitefully she was sure, had pointed out every billboard for McDonald's and Coca-Cola. That was what children remembered, not the British Museum or Rodin's drawings; what they remembered was the Guinness spilled into Daddy's lap, the pigeon with a deformed foot, free chocolates on the pillow.

"Morning, daughter."

Her father, sauntering between tables, handsome in white slacks, blazer, cravat flowering at the neck. He moved a touch stiffly as always, his pencil moustache precisely trimmed and his white hair combed back. "God, what's all that sun for?" he rasped, sitting down and crossing his legs. He peered at the other breakfasters as if incredulous that anyone could be up at such an hour.

"I need coffee."

"Did you sleep well, Dad?"

Her father just narrowed his eyes, as if to keep out the light. He hadn't slept well since Nora's mother died, but perhaps it was simply age. The waitress arrived, allowed this handsome old man to flirt with her, and went for coffee. How did he look so right, so at ease here? "You ought to eat something," she said. "You're getting too thin."

"My dear, I'm simply in fashion," he chuckled, lips barely parted. "The only thing I can digest first thing in the morning —"

"Is the news, I know. Where's Rose? I thought she was waiting for you."

"Yes, I found her sitting in the hallway outside my room just like a little orphan, that's what I told her. She watched me shave."

"She never watches Michael shave."

"Michael, Rose informs me, uses an electric razor."

"But where is she now?"

"I sent her to the kiosk to buy me a *Herald Tribune* and a packet of cigarettes."

"I can't believe this, Dad. You know I don't want you smoking around the kids."

"She likes doing errands for me."

This time the waitress's appearance didn't even elicit a glance from him. He picked up the cup almost as she set it down and closed his eyes for a moment. Before the trip they had seen her father only two or three times a year since he had returned to Montreal and the old, unrecognizable neighbourhood. He only taught part-time now, to "gifted" students as he put it, and he liked to joke that the other teachers treated him politely out of deference to his Russian accent and impeccable manners. As for Rose, Nora had never known a more serious child. Rose's first-grade teacher had even telephoned Nora to tell how her daughter shunned friendships with the other children. To Rose her grandfather should have been almost a stranger. But from the moment of their rendezvous at the Toronto airport Rose had taken to him and barely left his side. Nora's father, to her surprise, submitted to her presence. He slowed to her walking pace, talked in a reasonable tone, even occasionally held her hand. Nora discovered what could only be a previously hidden and ugly side to herself, for only that could explain her not being absolutely delighted.

"Rose doesn't like Hebrew school," her father said.

"But it's only her first year, and just Sunday mornings."

"I don't like to interfere but I'm afraid I couldn't help agreeing with her. What does she need it for?"

"That's pretty obvious, I should think. To learn about being Jewish."

"Ah," was all he said, and tipped back the cup of coffee. How he could make her furious. If her father wished to cling to whatever views he picked up in some dingy Moscow restaurant half a century ago that was his business, but to undermine what she and Michael taught their children was inexcusable. But what could she say —

"Hello, orphan."

Rose came running, through the trellis, past the other tables, and into her grandfather's arms. Chuckling, he patted her fraternally on the back. Rose wriggled around to sit between his white-trousered legs on the edge of the chair.

"Just think, making me wait all this time for my newspaper."

Rose was breathless. "The lady gave me a green package — menthol. But I know you won't smoke them, Grandpa, so I wouldn't take it. You should have heard her swear, in French but I could tell. She had to look on all the shelves."

For the first time Rose looked up at her mother, the corners of her mouth turned down, Nora leaned over to brush the hair from Rose's forehead, a reason to touch her. Of all the children Rose looked the most like her — the thin nose, high forehead, the dark crescents under her eyes.

"Rose, honey," Nora said, "you've got your shirt inside out."

"I don't care."

"Where's the waitress? I want to order you some breakfast."

"Grandpa doesn't eat breakfast."

"Grandpa is very stubborn. We love him but we don't agree with him. How about we order you some cereal and fruit?"

Rose didn't protest, her sign of acquiescence. Nora's father deftly tapped a cigarette from the package and drew a box of wooden matches from his blazer. "You'd better shift into the next seat, orphan," he said. "I don't want you to get my smoke."

"Smoking is bad," Rose said, pulling herself into the wicker chair.

"Yes, very bad."

"But won't it hurt you, Grandpa?"

"I'm ancient, it's too late for that. Just being alive hurts me."

"Please, Dad," said Nora.

"Your mother protests my small act of self-dramatization. She's right, of course. Ah, here's that pretty waitress."

Rose's breakfast was duly ordered and delivered and, once the strawberry halves had been arranged by her into a pattern whose meaning was necessary but obscure, she began to eat. Nora's father leaned back in his chair, cigarette held aloft, and scanned the newspaper's headlines. "I hope Michael is finding his excursions to town productive," he said.

"I think so. If you'd like to go in, I'm sure he'd love to take you tomorrow."

"Oh, I don't think so. It's rather pleasant here. No sights to see, no galleries to look serious in. Right, orphan?"

Rose looked up and smiled, her teeth red with strawberry.

"Not one bit of Canadian news," Nora's father said and rattled the paper. "We don't exist, we're still a few handfuls of snow. No, here's something, a profile of the West Edmonton Mall. Biggest in the world, apparently. That ought to boost our international image."

Rose inexplicably laughed and kept eating. She had wild hair that defied brushing and skin pale as wax. God, Nora loved her children, she loved Rose, but they made her — how, she hardly understood — afraid to show it, as if something fragile would fissure and crack. Rose looked up to make sure her grandfather was still there, and began to eat again, tipping the bowl to capture the last sweetened spoonful of milk. No, there really was nothing wrong, it was she who didn't appreciate all that she had.

"Nora, dear. Morning!"

Nora saw Malcolm Moriarty waving as he drew out a chair for his wife. Just when she did not want to move, but Malcolm Moriarty was the sort of man who treated bare acquaintances like the best of friends and meant it. Nora sighed. "Be right back," she said and got up smiling.

"How rude of us not to come over," Malcolm said. "We wanted to greet your father and your daughter, what is her name again . . ."

"It's Rose, dear." Dorothy Moriarty's apologetic tone was warm and polished from years of use. She had aged very handsomely, hair in white curls and a soft, highly coloured face. "What Malcolm is saying, or rather not saying, is that we would have come over if my silly knee hadn't been asserting itself all morning. He wanted me to sit down."

"Yes, that's it," Malcolm smiled broadly. The dip and rise of his vowels no doubt identified in just which English town he had been raised. "Dorothy suffers, you know, but not a peep out of her, she's not a complainer. You've got quite a father, Nora, he looks just the musician. I must have a chat with him about Ravel. I don't know a blessed thing about music but I do love Ravel."

"Nora, if you'd like sit down a moment. Your children have such interesting names and so diverse. There must be a story behind that."

There was a story, of sorts anyway, and the Moriartys, who really were sweet, listened with so much interest that as she spoke of her children Nora felt herself flush with emotion. Malcolm had introduced himself in the dining room last night after she and Michael had returned from Cannes. Malcolm's red hair had receded to the very back of his head and he had a scrubbed, shining scalp. They were such a nice couple, fussing over one another; childlessness seemed their one sadness.

"Dorothy must show you the things she bought in the market yesterday. Last year we went to the Costa del Sol, but talk about crowds. A rumour went along the beach — well it's true, Dotty — that someone had spotted human faeces floating in the water. The plumbing system can't take the numbers, you see. Now, in England . . ."

Nora listened, about cottage rentals in Penzance, the influx of hooligans to London, but in spite of her instinctive liking for Dorothy especially, she was conscious of her father and daughter at their own table and, as soon as she could, excused herself. The table had been cleared, although Nora had hoped for a last cup of coffee, and her father and Rose had pushed their chairs together to the point of touching. Rose, her bare legs pulled up beneath her, rocked slightly as her grandfather spoke, his cigarette held just before his lips. Nora's expectant smile of return, having gone unnoticed, seeped away, and she stood like an unwanted listener at a party while her father spoke in that calm and formal voice she had always known.

"Wait a minute and I'll tell you. Your mother used to wait on the front steps for me to come home. On our street there was always something interesting for a young girl to see. The houses had rails and stairways running up their fronts — that's how apartments were built in Montreal, because of fire. Our door was on the second storey and Nora used to look through the rails at the boys playing hockey below or the girls skipping rope. She could speak some French then, picked it up by listening. At the end of the street, three or four blocks away, there was a small church that no one outside the neighbourhood knew existed, and sometimes the nuns would walk past. Nora said they looked like angels. But when the street really looked its best was after the first snowfall. Nora would stand with her nose pressed to the window and watch the people come out of their doors with brooms and sweep the snow away. And she would ask, 'Why are they doing that, Daddy —'"

Nora fled; how else to describe the sight of a woman running flat-footed with her skirt flying, hands in the air as if someone were flinging stones at her? Down the path and into the garden, not the formal garden on the other side of the hotel with its immaculate bushes of cubes and spheres, but the "English" garden with its wildflower beds and dusty path, surrounded by an ivy-hugged wall. She stood against the wall to catch her breath, a hand stretched across her breast. Why had her father's talk been so distressing? She knew only that she could not breathe, as if they had somehow sucked away the air from around her. All she could examine rationally was that she and her father had in the last years been anything but close. Their arguments had started when she was a teenager, the break when she and Michael had flown to other worlds. If the arrival of the children had introduced a formal truce and even, eventually, cordial relations, not even after her mother's death had they settled their oldest resentments. What had made this separation hurt so much and for so long was the affection she had known from her father, and how she had adored and admired him. She had never felt that way again until Michael.

A bird, of a startling green, lighted on a branch and began to trill. Another appeared, duller, and the two chased one another about before skimming over the wall. A shame Eileen hadn't seen, she loved birds. Rose was afraid of them, they fluttered in her dreams. Nora began to think her reaction exaggerated and even to feel as if she had made herself ridiculous. After all, a mother should be glad when a daughter shows an interest in the mother's childhood. Hearing about those years in Montreal that Nora had forbidden herself to dwell on might even bring Rose closer to her. If only Nora could have patience. She had let the day get away from her again, but if she could just be a little stronger she could rescue it.

She was sitting on an iron bench and lacing on her sandal when the hotel dog, a woolly hulk with a flat smiling face that must have been the descendent of some obscure European breed, came pounding down the path, followed by her hooting twins, Gordon with his cap pulled to the side and Eileen waving a paper flag on a stick. The dog ran over Nora's feet but the twins stopped and stood before her in a little mushroom of dust.

"We want to go swimming but Ananda won't watch us even though he's just sitting at the pool writing in that dumb book."

"I was just coming down. You find Grandpa and Rose while I change."

"Mom," Eileen said, tracing a line on a path with her shoe. "I don't like my bathing suit."

"Why not?"

"It's too thin. I mean up here."

She pointed to her chest which was flatter than chubby Gordon's. So self-conscious already, the daughter of a generation that had tossed away its bras. "You can wear a T-shirt overtop," Nora said.

"That's a good idea. Let's go, Gordon."

"I'm going to wear a T-shirt too."

And they were off, back the way they had come.

Light everywhere, on the surface of the pool, on the pink deck that was as porous as coral, on the glittering rail that overlooked the cliff and the sea. Nora, a bathing suit beneath a tie-dyed shirt, squinted from her lounge at a view as bleached out as a colour photograph left in a window. She saw Eileen hugging herself by the edge of the pool as Gordon, still wearing his cap, threw himself over the water and accomplished his object of making a big splash. The cap came up first and beneath it a grinning Gordon. Closer to Nora sat her father, his trousers rolled up and his feet dangling in the water. A breeze from the sea crossed Nora's ears, bringing Rose's voice,

". . . but if Mommy was afraid of these boys . . ."

Nora turned her head, not wanting to listen, and saw the young man who acted as porter and, apparently, pool attendant, scurrying down the stone stairs balancing a tray of drinks. He distributed them to the tables pulled together by the family of Germans who were judging two of their wives in a diving contest. When the young man had one drink left he brought it to the chair beneath the umbrella where Ananda sat. Her son's hairless chest looked narrow next to the athletic man in his tight tennis shirt with the crest of the hotel on the pocket. They spoke for a moment until Malcolm Moriarty, sitting with his wife under the awning, called the attendant who, after taking their order, bounded up the stairs again.

Nora shifted the lounge so the sun fell across her face. With her eyes closed she could smell the sea and, when the breeze picked up, something stronger, like gutted fish and diesel fumes. The sound of wet feet slapping, voices in German and French, the faint whine of music.

"Quick, Mom, you've got to come."

She opened her eyes to see a dripping Eileen. "What's wrong?" The image of a child, Gordon, Rose, at the bottom of the pool, drowned.

"Gordon wants to show you something. I'm not allowed to tell what."

Eileen pulled Nora along, past the tables of Germans who were counting, "*Ein . . . zwei . . . drei!*" and then an arc of spray, down to the end of the deck where Gordon stood on a stool to peer through a telescopic viewer meant for spotting ships.

"Look at this, Mom. Topless."

"What are you talking about?"

When Nora looked through the viewer she could see the hazy image of a sun deck and two women who had laid their tops aside.

"Pretty funny, eh Mom?" Gordon said. "Who else can we tell?"

"It isn't necessary to tell anyone," Nora said, her hand already swinging the viewer towards the sea. "We shouldn't spy on people."

"Come swimming with us," said Eileen, wishing to make amends.

"Yeah!" said Gordon. "I want to go back in the pool."

"A swim would be nice. Let me just take off my things."

"Mom?"

"Uh-huh?"

Gordon pointed to the party of Germans. "Are those people really Nazis? Ananda says they have keys to our rooms and could come any time in the night and take us away."

"Ananda told you that? Jesus. You two go ahead and I'll meet you in the pool."

Back at her lounge Nora dumped her sandals and, pulling her shirt over her head, saw the world go pink and red. On her way to the pool she stopped by Ananda, who sat with the journal in his lap, sipping his drink from a straw. From above, Nora spoke to the bristly curve of his scalp. "I would appreciate you not telling your brother and sister nonsense about Nazis and God knows what else. Kids have a hard enough time understanding these things without being encouraged in stupid prejudices. If that's all you have to say then you better keep to your silent routine."

When Ananda looked up, Nora was shocked by how stricken he looked. "I'm sorry," he said.

"It's all right, you didn't mean it."

"But I did. Don't — don't — uh, I'm a shitty person, Mom."

"Ananda, how can I —"

But when she tried to put her arms around his shoulders he twisted away in his chair. "I'm going swimming," Nora said and headed for the pool. She walked to the deep end and slipped over the edge, the water passing over her legs, her breasts, her eyes.

She felt hands tugging at her and, opening her eyes, saw the bubbling grins of her two children, their hair wisps of seaweed. They all came up together.

"Let's play underwater charades," Gordon said, paddling furiously to keep afloat.

"Mom goes first," said Eileen.

"Yeah, and make it a hard one."

"You want hard?" Nora said. "You got it." And held her breath.

By the time Nora hooked her arms over the side of the pool and hung there she had little enough wind to spare for words. "That's it," she gasped as the twins bobbed beside her. "I'm waterlogged. You dolphins will have to cavort without me."

"Aw, Mom."

But Nora wasn't listening. She had seen Ananda, still under the umbrella, talking to the pretty waitress. Her tray was covered in empty glasses and she and Ananda were having a tug-of-war over his. Which meant, Nora realized, that even as she appeared to give him a lecture in French manners, their hands were touching.

"Everybody out," Nora said. "After we dry off it's time for lunch. A *family* lunch."

Rounding up the family, yanking dry shirts over their heads and herding them around a table on the café patio required the tenacity of a schoolmistress. And just when they had settled down, the hotel dog came lumbering across the café, to be pounced upon by the twins while Rose climbed shrieking into her grandfather's lap. Nora got the children seated again while the dog settled contentedly beneath the table so that she had to straddle it with her legs. "That isn't a dog," Nora's father said. "That's a rug in need of a beating." He looked, as usual, regal, hair wetted and combed back, cravat a perfect topsail. "Hmm," he mused, considering the menu. "On such a splendid day lobster seems appropriate."

Nora sighed; the children didn't eat shellfish. She kept a kosher house not from some religious superstition but to give the children what Michael called cultural definition. Her father, on the other hand, defied such signs of faith with the same glee he had felt as a sixteen-year-old music student newly arrived from the village. Rebellion made him nostalgic.

"What are you going to order, Ananda?" Nora asked.

"I'm not very hungry."

"But you didn't eat breakfast."

He shrugged.

"Ananda, please."

"All right, I'll have a hamburger."

"There's no hamburger on the menu. Can't you be a little adventuresome?"

"No."

"Look at this, Andy," his grandfather — who knew how he infuriated Nora by using that name — pointed to the menu. "I think this *steak frites* ought to be pretty good. Just like a hamburger only they forgot to grind it."

Ananda looked reluctant to give in. "Okay," he finally said.

"I want that too," said Gordon.

"And me," said Eileen.

"That was easy," said Nora. "What about you, Rose?"

"I want lobster," Rose said.

"Honey, lobster isn't kosher. Besides, you've never

eaten it and you won't like it."

"I want it."

Nora pressed her fingers against her brow. It was at moments like this that theories of child-rearing proved less than adequate. "I don't think so. You'll have what the other kids are having."

Rose fixed her mouth shut, a bad sign. Her grandfather leaned over.

"You can try mine, orphan."

"Don't interfere, Dad."

"I simply thought — well, you know best. Perhaps I'll indulge in a glass of wine."

From their side of the table the twins watched this drama in which they were not participants with their different proportions of fear and interest, but its finale was merely the waitress's arrival to take the order. Nora was not so preoccupied with Rose that she could not keep an eye on Ananda in the young woman's presence, but he did not even look up.

"Mom," Gordon said after lunch had arrived and he had stuck two fries under his lips to look like fangs, "Are we ever going to go to the beach?"

"Maybe Dad can take the afternoon off tomorrow and drive us. Does everyone want to go?"

"I do," said Eileen.

Ananda shrugged. "Sure, why not."

"How about you?" Nora said, running a hand over Rose's hair.

Rose shook her head.

"You don't?"

Rose tilted her head to look at her grandfather. He peered down at her through half-closed eyes.

Rose nodded. "Okay."

"Ah, the beach," said Nora's father. "Sand in your bathing suit" (the children giggled) "no bathroom for miles. That's my idea of paradise."

"Mom?" said Rose.

"Yes, love?"

"Do you think they have ice cream for dessert?"

"You know, I think I saw ice cream on the menu."

"Strawberry?"

"Sure," said Gordon. "And they also have cabbage flavour."

"Yech," said Eileen.

"And dog food flavour and medicine flavour . . ."

Rose laughing, Eileen banging her fork, the dog barking under the table.

"Nora," her father said, wiping the edge of his mouth with his napkin, "I am not related to these hoodlums."

If only she could have kept them around that table forever, but it was enough, that hour, she wouldn't ask for more. The twins ran off together to investigate a rumour that the pond in the formal garden was inhabited by a turtle; Ananda bounded away, hands buried in the oversized pocket of his shorts and the ties of his sneakers dragging behind; and her father and Rose got up together in silence, as if speech weren't necessary, like an old couple.

With the others gone the waitress dropped her smile and, leaving the chit among the table's debris, turned her back. Nora signed a generous tip and retreated to her room where she undressed by the afternoon light diffused through the sheers. The lunch had gone off so well and here she was, sitting on the edge of the bed, a breath away from weeping. It happened with an increasing frequency that terrified her. She was breathing quickly, gasping almost, and felt a rising curl of nausea. Think of something good; think of Michael. Those conversations in the college dormitory, late at night, when the deep regularity of his voice had soothed her out of loneliness. From those first days she had been grateful for Michael's interest in her; she still was, when he showed it. Remembering the book she had once read to the children over many nights, she wondered if she were like Tinkerbell, who, if she were not believed in, would fade and fade.

The telephone sounded, two short and foreign trills. Nora lifted the oversized receiver and held it to her ear.

"Hello?"

"Hi, sweetheart."

"Michael. I didn't expect you to call. Oh, I'm glad."

"I've just got a few minutes between meetings. If you thought this place was crowded yesterday — today it's a madhouse. But Nora, you won't believe who I met not half an hour ago."

Michael's voice sounded far away, as if he were calling from the end of a tunnel. "Who did you meet?" she said.

"You'll never guess."

"Please, Michael."

"James Bond."

"Who?"

"Come on, Nora, you know — Sean Connery. The

original. He's here promoting a new film. I couldn't believe it, he even signed an autograph for me. It was incredible. Nora?"

"I'm listening, Michael. When will you be back?"

"In time for dinner, so hold the kids until then. After we put them to bed we can have a little time to ourselves and straighten everything out. All right?"

"All right, Michael. Be careful driving."

"No problem, I'm getting to be a real pro with the shift. See you later."

After Nora hung up the receiver she lay down on the bed, head on the pillow, eyes closed, and whispered into the room, not a word but a sound. She was asleep. The light through the sheers grew dimmer; she did not move. When finally Nora stirred, the sensation was of pulling herself up from the bottom of a well. She groped for her watch on the dresser and stared, hardly believing that it could be almost seven. She must have been more tired than she knew; perhaps that had been the cause of her mood. Mechanically she sat on the toilet and then turned on the shower, first cool, and after the shock, hot. As her head cleared Nora even began to anticipate the evening if not with pleasure at least without dread; after all, the day so far really had been as fine as she had hoped. After the children had gone to bed she and Michael could sit in the bar and talk and she would order something nice, a glass of champagne. Nora brushed out her hair, put on stockings and slip, and shimmied into the evening dress that Michael had insisted she buy in Paris. And she who still preferred jeans and old sweatshirts stood in front of the mirror and had to admit that she looked ravishing. The dress was of heavy satin, large shoulders, a low neckline, belted at the waist and finished in a full skirt. Nora put on her heels, a silver necklace, and looked again. "My God," she said aloud, for she remembered the days when her father still gave concerts and Nora would watch her mother, who always accompanied him, standing before her own bedroom mirror, just like this.

Gordon and Eileen she found in their room, sprawled on the beds watching *Dallas* dubbed into French. "Where are Ananda and Rose?" she asked.

"I don't know," Gordon said without looking away from the television.

"Get dressed for dinner, you two. And we're eating in the dining room, so put on your good things."

"Aw, Mom."

"I want to see you moving."

She began a hunt for the others, through the hotel corridors, in the sitting rooms, even out to the café where the young athletic man was closing the umbrellas for the evening. It was while considering where to look next (and a gaggle of tennis players entering the lobby looked her satin figure up and down with, she was sure, amusement) that Nora looked through the revolving glass doors and saw Rose and her father, standing at the edge of the hotel drive, watching the cars coming back from the city.

Her father had always loved automobiles, and as Nora made her way down the drive, heels catching between bricks, she could see him, oblivious to the billows of exhaust, pointing at each arrival and describing its history and handling. "Well, hello there," Nora said, but a convertible gunning up the drive drowned out her voice and her father, who seemed not to have noticed her, kept talking to Rose.

"Now there's a nice Mercedes, you don't see that colour in North America. Reminds me of our first new car, '53 Dodge, a real beauty. We'd only bought used until then. Now those were real cars, the size of battleships. When I leaned on the horn all the neighbours came running and your grandmother brought Nora down the stairway. 'Is this your car, Daddy?' she said. 'Are you becoming a salesman now?' We laughed and laughed . . ."

Whatever Nora shouted, it made both her father and Rose turn and stare. After a moment her father said, "Yes, Nora?"

"Dinner. You have to get ready."

"Of course."

And Nora turned around, back to the hotel. She did not know where to go, or rather where to hide, and so she stood before the newspaper kiosk, so close that the words blurred before her eyes. She was now only this myth, a little girl on an iron stairway, and the Nora who stood before the papers was fading and fading, leaving only a satin shell —

"Without my glasses I can't see, only the big words."

The woman from Switzerland, the widow, appeared beside her, peering at the hanging newspapers to read the headlines. "Nothing so important, I think," she said.

"No," Nora said.

"Are you and your family having a good holiday?"

"Yes, thank you."

"They always treat me well. My husband, he was once printing the menus for the hotel, the bills, everything. He was demanding of perfection."

"You must miss him."

"This is natural."

"I don't know what I'm doing here," Nora said and raised her hand as if to stifle a laugh. "I'm looking for my son."

"The big one?"

"Yes, I have to go."

"I saw him just some time ago, on the upper level. I always take a room on the upper level. The stairway is good exercise."

"Are you sure it was my son? I don't know what he could be doing there."

"Perhaps he is making a friend."

Nora just looked at her and a moment later was tripping up the escalator, holding aloft her skirt. Why she was going after him, whether she would yank Ananda and the waitress apart if she found them — all she did know was that she wanted to slap them across their faces until her own hands became real again. The corridor of the upper level was more narrow than the others because of the angle of the cliff and as Nora looked down she realized that she had expected to know in which room Ananda would be. She started to walk, stopping to listen and try each door before passing on to the next; on one she pounded with the flat of her hand but received no answer. Before the second to last she paused and heard what might have been a moan or merely the scrape of a chair. She put her hand on the knob — the bolt was only half turned in the lock and with pressure slipped out — and opened the door.

When she had last seen her son naked she did not know. He was tense as a bow, kneeling before the still-made bed, the window behind open to the darkening Mediterranean. The young athletic man had neatly folded his porter's uniform and left it on the chair and as he sat on the bed he turned his head — apparently only he had heard the door — and looked at Nora with what seemed to her the most inconsolable grief.

When she returned to her own room she pulled a chair from the desk and for the next hour watched through the window as evening turned to night. The curving drive of the hotel was traced by merging circles of lamplight and the awning had turned a luminous gold. After a time the athletic man appeared in his uniform to relieve the doorman and when a car pulled up he would stride forward to open the door. What Nora felt about him, or her son, did not matter now; they were silhouettes turning end to end against the sea.

An arc of headlights appeared on the road and, sliding into the drive, became the mustard Citroën. Nora rose, paused before the mirror to brush her hair, and left the room. The whisper of satin accompanied her to the main level of the hotel, past the dining room where white cloth and crystal glasses waited. Gordon and Eileen came skipping from the lobby, dressed decently, and ran into the sitting room, from which she could hear the unmistakable touch of her father's hands on a piano, precise and formal. He was playing Scriabin, as he always did when he wanted to show off, and when Nora entered she saw a dozen enraptured guests. Rose, in a white dress and with a ribbon in her hair, sat on the piano bench beside him, watching not his hands but his stern face. Nora listened and when Michael came in from the opposite doorway she did not move but waited for his eyes to find her. When they did he smiled and mouthed across the room, so that she could read the words, *you look beautiful.*

# The Village
# Angel

I

Eugene Bett stood before the spotted mirror and, with his one hand, deftly knotted his tie. He considered with satisfaction how he had chosen the tie several years ago, neither too wide nor too narrow, so that it had never quite gone out of fashion. This evening he wore his gray suit (the other was blue) and if it had the cut of another time, an old man was hardly expected to keep up with changing style to that degree; indeed, it was almost expected that he cling a little to the appearance of the past.

Bett had a large face, almost regal, and strangers passing in the street sometimes halted, as if recognizing him from a picture in a magazine. Perhaps it was the white hair swept impressively back, the high forehead and clear eyes, the expectant smile. To be shown to best advantage, his smile required the neatest of settings: morning shave with razor and brush, shirts hung in the bathroom to steam out wrinkles, shoes briskly polished, the left jacket sleeve ironed flat and pinned into the pocket.

Bett took from the hanger his overcoat (which too had one sleeve pinned) and draped it over his shoulders in the European manner. From outside his door he turned the three locks and then started down the hall, which looked dismal even to Bett, whose habit was to put the best face on things. The landlord — not a man but a numbered company — refused to replace burnt-out bulbs or carpets worn to threads, and there was talk that each tenant would soon receive a notice of eviction.

The elevator had only three flights to rise but it took several minutes and continuously moaned. Its door had once been a mirrored gold, Bett remembered, but now the sheen was blistered and if one brushed against it a shower of rust would stain one's clothes.

He felt no impatience. Waiting was his profession, one that he might not have chosen but that he executed as if it were an art. The elevator door shuddered and Bett, who did not wish to get thumped when it suddenly shut, readied himself to spring in. But when it opened he held back, for Miss Drew was as quickly stepping out, enveloped in her balding rabbit coat. "Good evening, Miss Drew," Bett said in a voice that made even strangers smile. Only Miss Drew did not reply, but walked past with her face hidden in the folds of her kerchief. Bett disapproved of a young woman dressing as if she were old. Miss Drew had lived in the building for three years, but he still knew nothing about her. Occasionally the mailman put a letter for her into his box by mistake and Bett, whose own mail was invariably computer-generated, would stare at the handwriting on the envelope as if it were a human face.

The elevator took Bett down to the lobby. Its curving walls always reminded him of a fish bowl. He passed the two armchairs (which had mysteriously developed long rips up their backs a couple of weeks ago and were still unrepaired) and opened the glass door onto Third Street. Yesterday, spring had officially arrived, but this evening a surprisingly sharp wind blew from the Hudson. As getting his overcoat on properly now would be too great a struggle, Bett merely held it closed with his hand as he started to walk. Not hunched over but straight and firm, he was an impressive figure, broad-chested and almost military. A light snow swirled into the light of the street lamps and rushed to the pavement. A flake alighted under Bett's right eye and melted. When he groped for a handkerchief his overcoat flapped open.

He was glad to reach Broadway, with its lighted windows and neon signs and young couples bent over to read restaurant menus. Even in the cold he could smell the perfume of women and the spiced odours of Indian restaurants. He had long ago learned to enjoy the bustle of which he was not a part, and even to feel as if he too had somewhere interesting to go and people anxious for his presence. And, after all, did he not have somewhere to be in only a few minutes time, his own curtain-raising to attend? He had reason, after pausing for an ivory limousine to pass, to increase his stride with purpose.

On the other side of Broadway the street darkened

again, and a series of trashbins, covered in a film of snow, sparkled like a range of mountains. Bett descended a set of steps to a door, before which two women in wool coats stood chatting. He nodded, bringing two fingers to his temple as if to touch an invisible brim, and the women smiled as they let him pass. That moment alone could have sustained him for half a day, yet he had so much more to look forward to! He walked keenly through the foyer where children in various states of winter dress ran after one another, holding violin bows or sheet music. Bett had just enough time to slip into the men's room and stand before one of the enormous porcelain urinals, their inner walls stained the colour of saffron. He draped his overcoat on a hook and had begun to wash when a man in a handsome blue coat came in. The man stepped up to a urinal and Bett, putting on his elderly smile, said, "They don't make them that way anymore."

"I suppose not," the man said.

"The size of bathtubs!" Bett chuckled.

"Or coffins," the man joined in. "They're big enough to be buried in."

"Quite right!" But Bett frowned; he disapproved of morbid humour. Looking down, he noticed a spot on his trousers and needing time to let it dry, he let the man pass out of the lavatory before him. In the hall, lights flicked on and off and people scrambled through the double doorways. Bett enjoyed this last-moment rush as he entered the concert hall and took a place next to the man in the blue coat just as the lights went down.

The term "concert hall" was his own, for the room was

no more than a flattened box with several rows of benches along one wall and a few stage lights clamped to the ceiling pipes. When the lights went up an audible humming began and a thin man with a moustache appeared. "Welcome to our weekly student recital," he said. "Here is where we find the Casals, the Bernsteins, the Raimondis of tomorrow. May I remind those parents who have not yet paid for the spring semester to do so by the end of the week. You will find a program under your seat."

Although Bett knew the program was there, he always waited for this announcement, to increase the suspense of the evening. The first performer, he read, would play Satie's "Trois Nocturnes." A boy appeared on the stage and, without waiting for the applause to end, sat down on the piano bench and began to play. Bett was undoubtedly the most faithful of the recital followers (parents came only to hear their own children), and he liked to imagine that the teachers suspected him of being a scout for one of the music colleges. Certainly no one else came simply to hear Brahms played on a miniature cello by a tiny Oriental girl, which Bett enjoyed immensely. A wrong note might be struck, the tempo sped up, the composer's deeper meaning proven elusive, but Bett closed his eyes and took in, if not the particularities of each performance, then the principle. It was all music, heavenly music!

When the lights came up for the interval, Bett saw that the man in the blue coat had already drawn out his *Times*. Bett placed his large hand on his crossed knee and said, "The waltz was particularly good, didn't you think?"

The man's reluctance to withdraw from his paper did

not wilt Bett's patient smile. Finally the man said, "Yes, very good."

"Perhaps you have a child at the school."

"My son. He's playing in the second half. Trumpet."

"Where is this?" Bett scrutinized the program, and the man leaned over and pointed. "Ah yes, the fanfare. I shall anticipate it with pleasure."

"More than he will," the man said, and as he crossed his legs too Bett read the movement as a sign of intimacy. "The lessons are his mother's idea. We disagree about these things."

"I'm sure your son will execute his duty admirably. Still, performing before an audience can be hard for a young boy."

"That's what I say." The man folded his newspaper and turned on the bench. "Why make a kid go through that —"

"Yes, of course."

"— against his will. *You* can understand, but his own mother —"

The lights went down, but not before Bett gave a most sympathetic arch to his white eyebrows. "I will cross my fingers for your son," he whispered.

Even so, the boy performed miserably, halting and starting twice. Thankfully, the flutist and the singer who followed were superior, the latter giving a sweet rendering of several German *lieder*. All in all, Bett considered, a worthwhile, even stimulating, evening. When the lights came up he was disappointed to see that the man in the blue coat was gone. But the feeling was mitigated by the man having left his newspaper, which Bett slipped into his own inner pocket.

The snow had stopped and the city's countless heels had already erased any traces from the ground, although narrow lines still decorated the balcony rails like icing. Bett walked briskly in anticipation of the evening's culminating pleasure, and the first sight of the bright windows of the diner on Waverly Place made him swell with sociability. Luckily his preferred booth was vacant and he nodded familiarly to the cashier who was running a violet stick across her extended lip. The diner was clean, its pastries beneath glass domes looked admirably tempting, and the waiters did not make a solitary patron move to the counter except during the midday rush. Bett placed his overcoat on a hook and settled in the booth, from where he could gaze both down the aisle and out into the darkness of the street. It was a shame he had no one to speak to, when there were so many subjects one might discuss on such a night — for example, the relative merits of various Romantic composers, or the delights of a city in spring. Bett would have been happy simply to listen; indeed, he believed that his abilities as a confidant went sadly underused. But no matter, for Bett did not indulge in brooding or introspection, and he would satisfy himself with the ample pleasures permitted him every week at this time.

The waiter came to the booth, dressed in the starched shirt and black trousers of his trade. "The usual?" he asked, words that always had a splendid ring to Bett. The waiter closed his pad and, pointing a finger at the window, said,

"You see that? The hole there. It's from a bullet, yes, that's right! This morning, zing, right through the glass."

The waiter walked away and Bett, a little disgruntled, opened his newspaper. But instead of reading he gazed out the window until the waiter returned with the bowl of bread pudding and a teabag floating in a cup. The taste of the pudding, soggy and sweet, raised his spirits again, and the warm tea in his mouth brought him to a point of exaltation; a less self-possessed man would have found tears starting in his eyes. The tea, the warm tea!

Bett walked homewards as the delicate feeling carried him down the street. When he strolled with his hand in his pocket he looked, in the dark, like a whole man. Before his own apartment door he fumbled with the keys while listening for a sound from Miss Drew's across the hall. He often heard the television, or water in the sink, or even Miss Drew muttering to herself. But there was no sound tonight and he went inside.

Bett hung up his overcoat, replaced his shoes with a pair of slippers, and carried the newspaper to the living room. An hour later he loosened his tie, turned out the lamp, and retired to the bedroom, where he switched on the radio. With his one hand he could hang up his jacket, shirt, and trousers with perfect creases, and after performing his duties in the adjoining bathroom he lay on the bed and stared at the green dial of the radio. He could congratulate himself on a perfect day, without a single misstep.

II

"Can it be, Mrs Washington, that the new issues of the European journals have still not arrived?" Bett leaned slightly forward, smiling the cooperative schoolboy smile that he reserved for a certain kind of particularly difficult woman. Because Mrs Washington was black it was also necessary to show that his deference was untainted by condescension.

She looked up from her desk with annoyance, as if she did not hear this question at the same time every month, as if she had never seen Bett. "If they're not on the rack then they're not in," she said and gave back a humourless smile that was more like a tic.

"Yes," Bett nodded at the wisdom of her observation. "But it is already the twenty-second!"

Mrs Washington sighed. "Hold on and I'll look in the office. Something may have come in today's mail."

"You are extremely kind."

Triumphant, Bett waited at the desk. This moment of expectation was no less significant than the receiving of the magazines themselves. Like the other library patrons, Bett wore his overcoat to ward off the library's dampness. It was a small, red, turreted building, quaint but deteriorating. He had been told that the insufficient heat was due to a starvation of funds, but he suspected the real motive to be an attempt to dissuade lingerers. The library had no public washroom, which meant that Bett could not drink before coming, and when he left (always at four o'clock) he would take stiff strides to the nearby New School for Social Research.

"Just this one," Mrs Washington said and handed over a magazine. If disappointment fluttered for the briefest moment across Bett's face, he banished it with a look of gratitude. "I greatly appreciate your efforts as a professional."

"Anyway, they're cutting out all foreign subscriptions."

"How is that possible?"

"If you wish to complain I can tell you where to write a letter."

"Oh no, I'm sure they know what is best."

Bett returned to the reading room, only to find that he had neglected to save his place and would have to stand again until another came free. The other patrons wore not only coats but fur hats and gloves with the fingertips cut off. With the several regulars Bett had a nodding acquaintance: the woman with knotted hair who read books on chemistry and laughed soundlessly, showing the gaps in her teeth; the bald man who snipped passages from the *Wall Street Journal* and added them to a weighty ball of clippings held by rubber bands. Although they never spoke, the regulars often exchanged respectful nods, as if they were independent scholars ostracized for heretical views.

A chair came free and Bett moved to take it. The magazine given to him by Mrs Washington was always filled with photographs of the remnants of European royalty and pop celebrities caught topless on their yachts by telephoto lenses. The bald man across the table muttered and snapped a rubber band. Bett examined the magazine's cover and then turned to the first page.

After his afternoons at the library, Bett always walked down to the park. The temperature had surprised the radio weatherman this morning by dipping back below freezing — Bett had heard him taking a good deal of ribbing from the other newscasters — and as Bett's usual bench was layered in ice he moved to one closer to the arch. He had come prepared, shielded by a woollen vest and two pairs of socks, but his unprotected ears began to sting. Bett was not alone in the park; a man in a turban stood by the chess tables staring down at an empty board, and the pigeon lady had come with her paper bag. Most of the pigeons wouldn't leave their roosts and she was shaking her fist at the arch and calling out oaths.

Bett knew how a mind refused to stay empty. It demanded filling up, like a stove needing coal, inexhaustibly hungry. So he had kept himself busy, and even in repose had resisted his memories of the years before emigration, had fought them back with a vigilance that demanded the firmest will. Perhaps it was his growing age, or simple tiredness, but lately he had found images appearing of their own that he had once thought extinguished forever. Yet they had been so long suppressed that they seemed unreal, like the flickerings of some moving picture he had once seen and remembered only as a blur. They had given him an uneasy, half-sleepless night, and he did not feel quite himself today so that keeping to his routine required more than the usual exertion. He had almost given up his tussle with Mrs

Washington. But he had kept it up handsomely, and that, at least, was something to be proud of.

The few pigeons beat their wings against the ground and rose together, as if to charge the woman with the paper bag. They groped upwards and settled back on the arch. "Heartless!" the woman shouted. The word froze in the air.

On Saturday mornings Bett attended synagogue, either the reform service of Hebrew Union College on Fourth Street, or the Temple Emanu-El on Fifth Avenue. On Sundays he went to church: John Street Methodist, Fifth Avenue Presbyterian, St. Patrick's Cathedral. He often grew drowsy in the coolness and fell asleep, knowing even in slumber not to snore and disturb others.

This Sunday evening, when by habit Bett should have been preparing dinner for himself, he felt restless. He had the usual prospect of reading the weekend papers while listening to a radio phone-in show where callers raged about foreigners or called for a return of the death penalty to the state. And while this had been sufficient last week and the weeks before that, he found himself putting on his overcoat and heading for the diner where he allowed himself to go only on Wednesdays for tea. When he got there it was surprisingly crowded, and as his own booth was occupied by a boisterous party, he took the last remaining stool at the counter and ordered the dinner special and a carafe of red wine. As he held the glass under his nose, the scent of the wine alone seemed to intoxicate him. He ate his dinner — turkey with stuffing and beets — and listened to the hum of conversation that rose and fell around him like music.

Afterwards, he stood outside the diner, his wallet so unexpectedly reduced of funds, feeling himself sway ever so gently. He strolled home beneath drifting snowflakes, whistling under his breath and with the odd sensation that someone was waiting for him. Several times the sidewalk slid dangerously beneath his feet, but he finally arrived at the tattered awning of his own building, and he turned to the street and raised his head, as if to offer some vague blessing. He saw a bird suspended in the sky above the opposite building, dark and large. An eagle, perhaps. It plunged downwards, flapping enormous wings, and to Bett it was a pitiable sight struggling through the snow. Then he saw that the bird was falling towards him, and he held up his arm in defence. But one arm was not enough, and the bird pounded its sodden wings against his face.

Only it wasn't a bird; it was a newspaper. Batting it down, Bett felt utterly foolish, and he attempted to laugh should anyone be watching as he folded the paper — a hefty *Village Voice* — and tucked it under his arm.

Outside his own apartment door, Bett paused to catch his breath. Out of habit he listened to whatever sounds might be coming from Miss Drew's apartment. Of course he never meant to be intrusive, but there was always comfort in knowing that another being was going about her duties. Such sounds could even make him cheerful, and he felt that tonight, now that the effect of the wine had evaporated, a little cheerfulness was in order. He could hear the television and something else, rising and sinking again. Weeping. Quiet, grief-ridden. Listening, Bett realized with a shock that he had been waiting for months, perhaps even since her arrival, for an opportunity to speak to Miss Drew. The very possibility had sustained him all that time. But what he had half-consciously expected was a request for his assistance in unplugging a sink or catching a mouse, some act of minor chivalry. He had not expected weeping, and he hurriedly turned the last lock in his own door.

But no, that would not do. He ran his hand over his hair and gave Miss Drew's door a rap with his knuckles, rather louder than he had intended. The noise abruptly stopped and a moment later Miss Drew's voice came from so near the other side of the door that Bett jumped back.

"Who is it?"

"Forgive me for disturbing you, Miss Drew. I wanted to be sure that you did not need assistance."

"You just never mind."

"Yes. Well then, good night."

Bett opened his own door. He had performed the chivalry after all, and that Miss Drew did not appreciate it would not spoil his own sense of having done the right thing. The incident made him glad enough to retreat into the same silence of his own apartment that he had so recently fled. But a noise came from behind him and, turning, Bett saw Miss Drew standing in her doorway, wearing a terrycloth robe and with her hair pinned back, her face turned blotchy from crying. "I know, I look like something out of *Friday the Thirteenth*," she laughed giddily, though her allusion was lost on Bett. "You want to come in for a cup of tea?"

"It is good of you to be polite," Bett said. "But I invaded your privacy and must decline."

"Oh, that's crap. I've got nothing to do anyway until I can take this stuff out of my hair. Come on in."

Bett touched his invisible brim and followed her inside. The apartment had the opposite layout to his own so that he felt as if he had stepped into a mirror. "I've got a pot just made," she said, heading for the kitchen. "Irish Breakfast. I drink gallons, liquid is good for you. You take milk, don't you?"

"Yes," Bett said although in fact he didn't. He waited while she went into the kitchen, which, if it was like his, would be hardly bigger than a closet. Taking off his overcoat, he noticed that the sopping newspaper he had jammed into the pocket was making a wet patch, but not wanting to explain it to Miss Drew, he left it there. The big television had the sound on low. Bett gazed at its vibrant colours and realized that what lay behind the door across the hall would no longer be a subject for his speculation.

Miss Drew reappeared from the kitchen like a gorgon carrying a tea tray. They sat next to one another on the sofa and he felt stupidly surprised to discover that he had harboured some — some *feeling* for her, he could hardly say what.

"You're Beck, aren't you?" she said.

"Bett," he said. "Eugene Bett."

"Sorry. Tea's all right?"

He looked at the milky liquid in the cup. "Excellent, thank you. Miss Drew, I hope that your sorrow is not —"

"That's nothing," she interrupted. "Just the usual Sunday-night blues. It's a wonder I don't cry every night. You know, the thought of doing the whole week over again. Yech. I can hardly stand it."

"May I ask what you do that is so distressing?"

"Bank teller. Chase Manhattan, Upper West Side. You should try dealing with some of those rich bitches. Never say hello, always mad about something and blaming me like I own the bank. You know what they say? 'Listen, dear, my driver's double-parked on Columbus. Can't you go any faster?' And then there's my manager. A real pig. He's slept with half the tellers in the branch and resents me for telling him where to go. Always making excuses to drop by my apartment, like papers that need to go to the office in the morning. But his tricks don't fool me, I always tell him to slip them under the door. Once he said he needed to use the phone and when he got inside he pushed me right up against the television. I smacked him with an aerosol room deodorizer. Made him see stars. Can you believe it, he called his wife to drive into town and fetch him. I'd tell her what a letch he is if she wasn't such a cow. The only reason he doesn't fire me is that I'm the best employee he's got. I can do figures in my head, interest, mortgage calculations. He swears I'm going to get a promotion but I'm still waiting. Oh, how dumb — I've got a new bag of cookies!"

"No, it's hardly necessary." But she had already left him alone on the sofa. On the television he watched a small airplane dive into the roof of a house and burst into flames.

As she returned, Miss Drew undid the wire tabs of the package. "Double chocolate chip," she said. "Do you know anybody else in this building? I don't. They all seem like creepos to me. I won't use the laundry machines even during the day. I go down the street."

"Very prudent," Bett said, biting into a cookie and wondering how he might change the subject. "You have done your apartment very nicely."

"I know, and everything on sale too. Except for the TV, paid seven hundred dollars for it. I figure a person's got to have some pleasure in this life. You watch television? I prefer the soap dramas, *Dynasty*, *L.A. Law*, shows with continuing stories. It gives you something to think about until next week. I hate *Cosby*, everybody so happy, the perfect lovey-dovey family, who would believe that?"

Bett smiled vaguely as Miss Drew asked him to "do the honours" and pour more tea. When he tipped the pot the lid began to slide. "You have to hold it down with your other — oh," Miss Drew murmured. But Bett managed with an outstretched finger and Miss Drew, despite a giggle, expressed no curiosity over his missing limb. "You lived in this building before I moved in," she said, as if to tell him a fact. "If it wasn't rent stabilized you'd never catch me in this neighbourhood. I won't go into the restaurants — with all those queer waiters, who knows what you'll catch? Anyway, it's better to keep to yourself. In this city you can choose your friends from the sick, the very sick, and the ones who ought to get the electric chair. Did you hear the rumour that they're going to tear down this roach motel and put up condos? I hope they do, it'll give me the push I need to get out of here. Not just the neighbourhood but the city, maybe even the country. You've got an accent, from Europe or somewhere, I bet you've lived lots of places. There's got to be some place better than this."

Bett had no alternative to offer, but a sense of decorum kept him chatting for another half hour before he could rise to say good night. She accompanied him to the door and Bett, as he backed out, made a slight bow from the waist. "You'll come back again," she said, a command rather than an invitation. "I don't think you're the type to try anything. Now when we meet in the elevator it'll be different."

Yes, it will be different, Bett thought as he let himself into his own apartment. He felt as tired as if he had run several miles in heavy clothes. His apartment did not feel like the refuge he had been anticipating, but like some uninhabitable cave. As he slumped into the armchair he wanted to fall away from Sunday evenings and weekend newspapers and the moon of Miss Drew's face. But he didn't fall away, he just sat there huffing a little, and after a while he drew the wet newspaper from his coat.

### III

On Monday morning Bett walked to the telephone booth at Thompson and Third Streets and fished out the quarter he had placed in his overcoat pocket, along with the scrap torn from the *Village Voice*. The advertisement had appeared in the classified section, to which Bett had turned after exhausting the rest of the paper.

ANGEL WANTED — DYNAMIC YOUNG
THEATRE GROUP NEEDS BACKER FOR
FIRST PRODUCTION. THIS IS YOUR CHANCE
TO BECOME INVOLVED IN THE ARTS.
SERIOUS CALLS ONLY.

Bett dialled the number and after half a ring heard a click and then a deep, almost lethargic voice: "Thanks for calling the Genesis Theatre Company. No one can take your call right now but if you'll leave your name and number our director, Adam Frutkin, will get back to you. Today's question is, Is it theatre if no one is watching? Please wait for the beep."

Bett hung up. The recording had sounded both intimidating and ridiculous, and when the tone sounded he did not know what to say. Despite the temperature having dropped a degree from the day before, he walked to the park where, from his bench, he watched a postman pushing his cart down a path. The sky was a faint blue, as if a drop of colour had been mixed in a can of white paint. Bett would have liked to paint the ceiling of his bedroom that colour, so that at night he could feel as if he were floating in the sky. After some time he saw an ambulance rumble into the park, its light revolving leisurely. It halted with a jerk and two men took out a stretcher. They placed on it a form that Bett had not noticed lying on the ground. Then the ambulance drove off again, through the legs of the arch.

In the afternoon Bett went to the library. The woman who laughed to herself and the bald man with his ball of clippings from the *Wall Street Journal* sat at their usual places, too involved in their reading to look up. No more European journals had come in, so Bett spent his time holding a small copy of Virgil's *Eclogues* and gazing out the window onto Sixth Avenue.

In the late afternoon, the streets clogged with people rushing to their health clubs or to catch commuter trains, Bett returned to the telephone booth on Thompson Street and dialled again. Since this morning the door of the booth had been torn off, leaving just the hinges, and he had to press the receiver against his ear to muffle the sound of traffic. "My name is Eugene Bett," he said after the tone. "I am interested in becoming a supporter of the arts." Should he say more? He could leave no phone number, and so, after a pause, he slowly hung up the receiver.

Back at his apartment, he boiled a chicken leg for dinner and spent the evening listening to swing music on the radio. Though he wasn't tired he went to bed early, lying in his undershirt and looking up at a ceiling that was not blue like the sky but a rather soiled tan.

He heard a knock on the door.

"Bett, are you home? It's Doris Drew. I've made some tea."

Bett kept still until he heard the sound of her door closing. Then he rose, dressed again (even putting on his tie), and quietly left his apartment. By now he could recall the telephone number by heart, and as soon as he reached the booth he dropped in the quarter.

"Hello?" came the voice at the other end, the same as on the message.

"Good evening, I hope my calling is not inconvenient. My name is Eugene Bett —"

"Eugene Bett! I've been trying like crazy to find your number. I've been in agony."

"Yes, it's unlisted."

"Sure, that's what I guessed. We're very pleased that you're interested in the Genesis Theatre Company, Eugene. And I would be honoured to explain personally our goals, our objectives. I know you'll see how serious, how *dedicated* we are. Maybe we could meet, say over coffee —"

"I must tell you, Mr Frutkin, that as of yet I have simply, let us say, an interest. That is all."

"Of course. You're being straight with me, I appreciate that. And I'm impressed by *your* seriousness, Eugene. But an interest is something, a window, an opportunity —"

"Quite so —"

"When would be convenient for you? As far as you're concerned I've got no conflicts. My schedule is wiped clean."

"Mine is a little more difficult. Let me have a look." To Bett's own amazement he found himself thumbing the pages of a newspaper that had been left on the shelf. "I'm free tomorrow afternoon at two."

"Magnificent. You'll be uptown, I expect."

"No, in the village, actually."

"Perfect, that's where we're based. How about the Café Europa on MacDougal. It has the right atmosphere. Creative."

"Very good, Mr Frutkin."

"Call me Adam. Eugene, this feels to me absolutely historic."

Bett had passed the steamed windows of the Café Europa countless times, but he had never been inside, and opening the door he might have been entering a different neighbourhood from the one he had lived in for so long. He heard the clattering of cups, the hiss of the coffee machine, and he stared at the young people at their small round tables, speaking heatedly or pausing to stare with their journals open. If Bett had any second thoughts they came too late, for a figure was already rising towards him. The man was not what Bett had expected from the deep and languid voice; he was too young, too short, and too curly-headed. "Eugene?" the young man said, stretching out a hand. He wore a corduroy jacket, an iridescent tie, jeans, and running shoes. Noticing Bett's empty sleeve he smoothly exchanged one outstretched hand for another without any loss of eagerness. "Come and sit down. I'm Adam. It's great to meet you."

Bett balanced himself on the wire-back chair. "This place is very picturesque," he said.

"It's a good place to talk." Adam rubbed his narrow, unshaven chin. "I use it as a sort of office, a second home. Here's Marissa — she's an institution here. Marissa, I'll have another espresso."

"Please, have something to eat," Bett said.

"Well, maybe a little sweet. A cannoli, Marissa."

Bett ordered tea. Adam leaned back in his chair, stretching his legs under the table and closing his eyes for a moment, as if he were falling asleep. But he sat up again and leaned towards Bett with his elbows on the table.

"You love art, Eugene."

Bett stammered. "Yes, of course."

"Otherwise you wouldn't be here. You're a busy man, with obligations. Only a person with genuine passion could have phoned us. That isn't to say we haven't gotten other calls — several, in fact — but they wouldn't do. Uh-uh. They had only one thing to offer us, Eugene."

"Hmmm," Bett said.

"Money."

"Naturally."

"And money isn't enough. The Genesis Theatre Company is not going to be some tax dodge for a businessman or a plaything for his bored wife. That's not what our theatre needs. We need support, sure, solid material support. But the question is, at what price?"

"The price can be too high," Bett said.

"You understand. Money doesn't come without strings. Money is never innocent."

"Never," Bett confirmed.

"On the other hand," Adam slipped his hands behind his head and smiled, "we don't live in a dream world. This ain't utopia yet — money's not obsolete." Bett joined him in a little laugh. "Our company needs it just as much as the Broadway moguls. Only a fraction the amount, God knows, we don't throw money around when half the world is starving. We're frugal. But if we must have money and that money is, well, offered to us, we have to ask what sort of knowledge it carries. And that's what I have to ask you, Eugene."

Bett found his chair tipping to one side. The waitress placed their cups on the table along with Adam's pastry and the cheque. Bett watched Adam pour a stream of sugar into his espresso, jangle his spoon, take a long swallow. He admired the young man's nonchalance; Adam made Bett feel special just sitting at the same table. Evidently an answer to the question was not immediately required. Adam took in a deep breath and gazed hard at some point in the distance, as if he had withdrawn from the room.

"Ever read Rimbaud?" he asked.

"No, I haven't."

"Neruda? Jung? Eugene, you might be thinking, 'Shouldn't I be asking the questions?' Or maybe neither of us should. What we need is dialogue, a common ground. Okay, so we're both lovers of art. Big deal. Maybe we don't even mean the same thing by the word. Let me say what I think you don't mean. You don't mean those international theatrical monsters that need million-dollar sets, laser beams, roller-skating rinks, helicopters. That's Roman spectacle, barbarism at its worst."

"No, I don't mean that," Bett said. "That's just what I don't mean."

"Great. Though I'm not surprised. But there's something else I think you don't mean, Eugene. Theatre that's on the other end of the scale, but that's just another kind of marketing. I mean the performance in some SoHo storefront where the actors make animal grunts as the playwright burns a photograph of his mother with one hand and yanks himself with the other. That's just another form of elitism, daring us not to understand, or feel, or care. I don't think that's your idea of art either, Eugene."

Adam paused to bite into the pastry, showering flakes over the table. "That is just the dilemma," Bett said heatedly, as if he had been long possessed of this conviction. "When a person is dismayed by both one and the other. He feels tempted to give up."

"That's just it. We don't want you to give up. We don't want anybody to. But how can a person not feel doubt about the relevance of art these days? All you have to do is watch the news, right? It makes theatre seem superfluous, usurped by everyday events. A man obsessed with an actress shoots the president — that's a bigger story than anything she might act in. Or how about a religious leader of millions being exposed as sex-crazed? Or people convinced that Elvis Presley is living on a spaceship? Theatre's been left behind. And it's not just that theatre's been lost, we're all lost. We both know how insane this very city is, where the lawyers and the brokers are more dishonest than the drug dealers. How can theatre be anything but useless? A bunch of kids playing make-believe, that's all. Wouldn't it be better for us to spend our time helping even one hungry person, or a mother and baby without a place to sleep? Maybe even that's too late, when there's nothing out in those streets but hate. We might as well call it quits."

"But we can't do that." Yet it was strange: while Adam spoke with conviction he looked anything but despondent. In fact, he looked rather pleased with himself, and quite content in the warm café. Bett decided to be reckless. "For all you say, you don't hate the city."

"No, you're right." Adam smiled softly. "I wouldn't

live anywhere else. A crazy paradox, I guess. Of course, I'm not from here and maybe that's why. I'm Canadian, a refugee from Toronto. My family is very big in dry-cleaning back there. I was an advantaged kid, you know, music lessons and summer camp, trips to Europe. I was a kind of exile in a world of privilege. Naturally they don't understand why I want to live here, but I say you have to go right to the heart of darkness. Anyway, I'm here now."

"And you're not giving up on theatre."

Adam laughed. "No, I'm not giving up. You're great, Eugene, I can't wait to tell the others about you. I still love theatre, I'm crazy about it. I believe we can't live without it, that it can still save us. I'm excited as anything about what we're going to do. And I'm starting to feel that maybe you're going to do it with us. Here, I want you to take this —" Adam leaned down to his knapsack, coming back with a folder in his hand. "Take a look at these. But Eugene, I think we should be straight with each other. Are you still interested?"

Bett cleared his throat. "Yes. Yes, I am. To speak honestly I am hardly an expert on the theatre. I have not been, as you might say, behind the curtain. But I am most interested in your company. And at this point in my life I am looking for something more than just another business opportunity."

"I understand," Adam nodded. "You know, there's too big a gulf between the old and the young these days. Eugene, I want you to meet our company. For almost a year we've been working together. Really sweating. We're more than a company, we're like some post-nuclear-destruction family. For the longest time we thought that we were the only people left on earth, and it's as if we've suddenly discovered that there are other survivors out there. That's our audience, Eugene, all those survivors. We're ready to give them something they need as badly as food and water. We want to do a first production. The script is ready and I know the company is too. But frankly, Eugene, we need an angel."

Bett put his hand on the cheque. "I'm no Rockefeller," he said. "But I'd like to do my part."

⁓

The newspaper sellers in their corrugated sheds, the window mannequins in leather, the piles of melons in front of the groceries were suffused with an unusual pink glow of dusk as Bett walked the streets of the village, reluctant to return home. Finally, he arrived at his own door and stood in the hall brushing the snow from his shoulders and patting the damp top of his head with a handkerchief. He was tired but wide awake, and instead of going to bed he sat down in the armchair, with the folder that Adam had given him (and that he had protected beneath his overcoat) in his lap. He had always scrupulously avoided sitting this way, without a newspaper or music from the radio for occupation, alone among the shadows that stretched across the floor. During the worst years, those of the war and after, he had been confused and anguished; now in his last years he was merely confused and dull. His own story could not be told to a young person like Adam, who expected heroism or tragedy as a matter of course. For he had simply done what he had to, and survived, which he admitted was a kind of crime. A part of him had been lost, but it was merely a small piece when one considered it, a fragment of a fragment. Since then he had lived a quiet life, grinding but fortunate, and it had left him, finally, alone in this apartment. He had been endlessly patient, without the expectation of what patience might bring, but now something had changed. He could no longer tolerate the sweet taste of bread pudding in a glass.

Bett got up from the chair, leaving the folder behind, and went out the door to the hall in order to knock upon Miss Drew's door. He had avoided her all week, waiting in the morning for the sound of her retreating footsteps so as not to meet her at the elevator. He was not sure why he stood there, unless it was a sense of kindness — but that reason seemed a little thin now. Did he *want* to see her? Before he could think of an answer, before he could even knock, the door swung open and Miss Drew stood before him, brandishing a baseball bat in the air. Bett took a step backwards.

"Hooh!" she exhaled, her face losing its grimace, although she still held up the bat. "I thought you were a thief, or something worse."

"My apology for frightening you, Miss Drew. Are you all right?"

"Sure, what do you think?" She gave one of her chirping laughs and slowly lowered her arms. "Come in, I've just brewed a pot of tea. A good thing I saw who you were, I might have turned your brain to mush." She laughed again.

Bett dutifully followed her inside. "Forgive me, Miss Drew, but if you were suspicious should you not have stayed inside and telephoned the police?"

"Do you know how long it takes them to show up? Last year I took a course in self-defence. If anybody tries anything I'm going to do some damage. Sit down while I bring in the pot."

Bett obeyed, turning to watch the soundless television screen. The apartment was even neater than on his first visit and new plastic placemats had been set on the coffee table, perhaps in honour of his now-expected visits. Miss Drew returned with the tray and after fussing with the plates and spoons sat in the chair opposite the sofa, smoothing down her sweatshirt, which was imprinted with a Valentine heart enclosing the name of the city. Bett felt uncomfortable when she looked up at him, as if she were scrutinizing his face to determine where he had been. "I was out of town for a few days," he said. "On a business matter."

"Yeah?" Her face softened. "I was wondering, because I called on you once or twice. It was stupid, but I thought maybe you were hiding from me. Oh, I know I'm not the easiest person to talk to — plenty have told me that to my face. But is it my fault if I can't be a hypocrite like most people? If I don't like somebody I show it. And why should I like most people, anyway? It's easier to like dogs or horses. What do you think of the tea? I make it like they do in England. First you have to warm the pot. In restaurants they don't know how to make tea, that's why I never go."

"It is excellent," Bett said. "The best I've ever tasted. I understand now that brewing tea is an art."

"Well, I wouldn't go that far." Her gaze drifted towards the television set. "Must be nice to get out of town. The only time I've been away was last summer, when I went home for my mother and father's funeral."

"How terrible," Bett said, and then, "Do you mean both of them?"

"Uh-huh," she nodded. "Boy, was it a hot day, all the women sweated right through their dresses. Beside the cemetery there's this big field of sunflowers, stretching for miles. All those rows and rows of flowers the size of heads — they're just about the most ugly flowers on earth, don't you think? Afterwards, back at the house, nobody ate, it was so hot. They drank like fish, though. Ran out of ice, then whisky, and then gin. Everybody knew my brother was going to do it, he told every person in town. But the police never did a thing, that's why I know how useless they are."

Bett spilled some tea in his saucer. "I don't know what to say."

"I wish he hadn't done it," she laughed. "One day, when I've saved enough money, I'm going to move back and take care of him. I think they'll let him out if I swear to look after him, don't you? That won't be for a while, though, and now that they've given us notice we'll all have to move out."

"Notice?" Bett was unable to keep up with her.

"Are you kidding? The eviction notice. It's in every- one's mailbox, didn't you get yours?"

"I must have forgotten to check."

"We've got two months to get out, can you believe

those crooks? I may not like this rathole, but at least I can afford it. Of course they're being real nice by giving us first chance to buy a new apartment. Maybe they expect me to rob my own bank. Nothing to do about it, though. Those guys have truckloads of lawyers."

"Miss Drew," Bett muttered, "I am so sorry —"

"Don't be sorry for me, I'll land on my feet. You're the one who better start looking for a new place to live. It's people who don't face reality that end up living on the street."

∾

In his apartment, Bett got down on his knees with difficulty and laid the contents of the folder on the rug. Nine shining photographs. He examined the face in each photograph closely, Adam Frutkin's and the eight others he did not know. He arranged them into different patterns until he began to feel as if he knew them. Each face seemed to him remarkably beautiful.

## IV

A bulky paper bag tucked under his arm, Bett banged awkwardly on the steel door. He had walked to Canal Street humming a melody once heard played by an eight-year-old violinist, the hum growing louder and his step quicker the further he got from his own apartment. From behind the door came what he described to himself as the sounds of friendship — the most musical sounds he had ever heard —

and as the door opened and Adam clapped him on the shoulder, Bett felt as if he were shedding one life and entering another, as tender as a new infant.

"Eugene, come in, everybody's buzzing to meet you," Adam said. Behind him bobbed other faces that looked to Bett as familiar as if he had seen them in a dream, as if they were the faces of lost loved ones.

Despite the welcome, Bett resisted when someone tried to take the paper bag from his grasp. "My mistake," said a female voice and Bett saw a young woman with pale red hair. It was her photograph he had looked at the longest, kneeling on the floor of his living room. Her hand touched his arm. "You hold onto your bag if you want to," she smiled. Such a voice; Bett felt himself grow weak; he held out the bag. She took it gently from him, as if he were a child. "I'll put it in a corner where it'll be safe and sound."

Someone else lifted Bett's overcoat from his shoulders. Music was thumping from somewhere down the long space. He recognized all the faces now and saw that what made them beautiful without exception was their youth. It was Bett who appeared foreign among them, but their unrestrained handshakes and smiles made no acknowledgement of that, or rather did nothing *but* acknowledge this difference. Bett nodded and tried to speak a few words, but nothing came out.

"There's no rush," Adam said. "We'll all get to know one another. Jeremy, set up those chairs, will you? Eugene —" he joined his arm in Bett's "— we have a little show for you. I'd like you to meet E. G." They turned to a woman with straight bangs and small, wire glasses. She wore a man's big shirt and a loose tie. "E.G. is our resident play-wright. She's the author of the play we want to produce."

"Not author," E. G. said. "More like *collaborateur*." She gave the French pronunciation with a laugh.

"We'll sit here," Adam said, steering them towards three folding chairs that had been placed before the dark windows. The studio appeared to be an old industrial space. "The company talked the other night and felt that the best way to introduce ourselves would be to show you a little of what we can do. So each of our actors has prepared a monologue. Very brief, an exercise. E. G. helped them choose and I worked with them, but we haven't polished." Adam rubbed nervously at his chin, but E. G. looked absolutely serene. Adam said, "Nobody here is afraid to risk and fail, maybe that's what you'll see. Whatever else, we want this to be a moment of honesty. Okay," he nodded to one of the actors.

The studio went dark. Bett heard the sound of shuffling movement, then quiet, and then the lights came on. There was no stage but just the floor, upon which the seven actors stood, or leaned against a cast-iron pillar, or sat cross-legged, or lay down. First one spoke and then another. Each stayed in his or her place; there was no movement but only the voice and the more subtle expressions of the body. Each was its own performance, hushed or intense or rambling or lyrical. Bett recognized a few of the speeches — from Chekhov or the Old Testament or Shakespeare — but others were more modern and strange. Once he was star-tled by an outburst of shouting, and another time by hysterical tears. Bett had no idea how to judge each actor, or even if he liked one more than another. That they should perform solely for him was almost overwhelming, and whether it was that or the performance itself that took his breath away he couldn't have said, but he had to remind himself to breathe. And then it was over — and the lights went down and up again.

The actors, still in their places, blinked or shook themselves and stretched, as if emerging from sleep. Bett stood up — his legs pushed him up of their own accord — and if he had two hands he would have applauded, but instead he beat the flat of his hand against his chest, as if attempting to revive his heart. "Marvelous, marvelous," he gasped. "I . . . don't have words." Adam and E. G. stood up too and, grinning now, clapped vigorously. The actors took each other's hands and came forward, beaming as they started to chatter. "Come, we need introductions," Adam said, and put his hand against Bett's back — an electric shock — to lead him to the actors, who had formed a ragged line before the acting space.

One after another the women kissed Bett and the men shook his hand: Ramona, a heavy young woman with a piercing voice who flooded words over Bett so rapidly he could hardly take them in; Adrian, the youngest-looking male, wide-mouthed and with a bobbing Adam's apple; Miriam, with her thick hair and her curtsy; the monotone Annette; Vincent's dark stare and fierce handshake; Jeremy, soft-voiced, thin, and with a tuft of beard; and Jessica, of red hair and eyes so blue they seemed transparent, who put her arms around Bett and hugged.

"Let's bring out the food," Adam said, and Adrian and

Jeremy pulled out a table that had been collapsed against a wall. "I managed to get the Hunan place across the street to donate some eats to the cause. We were hoping this would be a celebration."

"I have been hoping so as well," said Eugene. "That is why I brought this —" and from the corner he picked up the paper bag and drew out an oversized bottle of champagne. The company set the table between two pillars, laid out the food, and cheered as Adam sent the champagne cork arcing through the air.

Ramona insisted on loading Bett's plate with rice and noodles as she recounted the company's history. "Adam gave acting classes and all of us were students. Can you believe it, he was only a few months out of school and already he was teaching others. He'd only been assistant director to one show, off-off Broadway, but it didn't matter because he was so good. Like Strasberg, but not a purist. We practise Stanislavsky, butoh, commedia dell'arte, Artaud, you name it. At first we were just students in different groups, but then he asked us each to join a special class. It's hard to say when we stopped being students and became a company. It just happened. Adam is amazing. Before him I didn't really know what acting was."

Bett felt as if he were being passed from one member of the company to another, from Ramona to Vincent to Annette. Jeremy wanted to discuss the motivation for his monologue and spoke with the quiet intensity of the confessional. But before he could finish, Bett was taken away by E.G.

"Bringing champagne was very generous," E.G. said as

she handed him a full paper cup. "And very ostentatious." Bett felt himself blushing like a schoolboy. To pay for the bottle he had sold a coin that he had once carried across two borders in the sole of his shoe. "It is not my regular habit," he said. "I am usually a frugal man. Would you tell me something about this play you wish to put on? I am eager to hear."

"So is the company," she said. "Adam and I have kept it a secret, so as not to distract the actors from their preparation. But we're ready now."

"To work together, you and Adam must have the same — what is the word? Vision." This venture into unknown territory made him giddy.

"Yes, I would say you're right. Not that our approaches are identical. Adam is more visceral, his nature is to act before thinking. Mine's more cerebral and abstract. I see in words, he sees in pictures. We're complementary."

"They're a couple of lions," said a voice behind Bett as a slim hand rested on his shoulder. It was Jessica. "What I think is that they're attracted by a mutual ruthlessness."

E.G. gazed at Jessica through her wire glasses. "And you, Jessie, are a little lamb."

"Well, don't eat me up. What's E.G. been telling you, Eugene? Isn't she brilliant? I'm terrified of E.G.'s brain. She's read all those French and Germans, and I can't even tell you what semiotics means! But you know how to really get to her? It's so sweet, she becomes just like a kid when you call her by her real name."

"Jessica —" E.G. warned.

"Oh, come on, I think it's a nice name. Elizabeth

Gertrude." The two women laughed and kissed on both cheeks. "Anyway," Jessica said, "Adam says I don't have to understand because I'm so fresh."

"Adam, bless him, is a latent chauvinist," said E. G.

"That's what I said! But we love him even more for it, don't we E. G.? And he's a great director. He opens up incredible possibilities."

"I hope you're talking about me," Adam said as he came between the two women and took each around the waist. Bett felt faint from the casual embracing, the sensation of the physical around him. "I've gone around to get a sense of everyone's performance experience," Adam said. "The company felt good with you watching, Eugene. Energized. Every artist in some way gives up the family he was born into. He chooses another, one that's not based on accident but on empathy and passion. Without that, an artist is alone, drifting."

Jessica stood up on her toes and kissed Bett on his cheek. "I feel you're one of us," she said.

∽

In the Café Europa, Bett assumed the stern countenance that expressed how deeply impressed he was by the solemnity of the occasion. Adam had brought along Jeremy who, despite his artistic little beard and striped vest, had been an accounting student before dropping out for acting. Beyond the window, snow fell and Bett felt as if there were no outside at all, as if the Café Europa were merely a stage set swirling in a never-ending whiteness. But Jeremy's papers were worldly enough, with their severe headings and columns of figures.

"We've worked hard to bring these figures down to manageable levels," Jeremy said as he lay the papers on the table. "It hasn't been easy, but as Adam likes to remind us, putting on a show like this is an exercise in discipline. We've cut out some large expenses. For example, the actors aren't to be paid until the show opens. The only company salary before opening night is Adam's. Five hundred dollars. A token really, Adam didn't want it but the rest of us insisted."

"You were right to," Bett nodded. Adam made no acknowledgement, but gazed towards the back of the café. "Here you can see the breakdown of major expenses," Jeremy continued. "First is the theatre. We've found a nice, small house on Eighteenth Street for a thousand a week, or four thousand for one week of setup and the initial three-week run. That's the minimum needed for reviews to get out and make the show a success so we can extend the run. Here you see the rental of lighting and sound equipment, set production, costumes and make-up, insurance. Over here we have the promotion costs. Found ourselves a real publicity wiz, she knows Frank Rich at the *Times* person-ally and guarantees we'll get coverage. The rest is for posters, flyers, advertisements, mailings. Putting on the show is only half the battle, right Adam? Everybody's clamouring for attention in this town and if you don't blow your own horn nobody will know you're even breathing. We've all heard those horror stories of shows that didn't get a word of press."

"That would be terrible," Bett said.

"Over here are salaries, minimum wage after opening night for the company plus two crew, with an escalating scale depending on box-office take. You can see this budget has been cut to the bone, we couldn't shave it any finer. To put it in round figures, the show will come in at thirty thousand dollars. That's a bargain."

Jeremy put down the coffee spoon that he had used as a pointer and stroked his beard. Bett had followed closely the figures, admiring their concreteness; his nods of approval were not forced but genuine. Now he looked to Adam for his expected pitch (wasn't that the term?) on behalf of his show. Adam did turn to look at Bett, but it was instantly clear that he had nothing more to say, that the previous conversations and the company's performance were enough. They had given Bett everything, had laid down their faith, and now it was for Bett to play the part of the generous and rewarding angel. But instead of speaking, Bett looked away. The snow fell so heavily against the windows that a muffled beating could be heard, as if wet burlap bags were being tossed against the glass. The three men sat at the marble table for minutes, for a quarter of an hour, for longer. The waitress, Marissa, approached and turned away. The coffee cups started to rattle — Jeremy's shaking knee under the table — and became still again. Adam remained motionless, his mouth so taut that if someone were to touch him lightly on the shoulder, Bett imagined, he would spring into the air. What surprised Bett the most was his own intense and painful interest in the uncertainty of what might happen in each passing moment. He hoped this was not cruelty on his part, but would it not be more cruel to end the hopes of these young people with a single word? Perhaps some unforeseen solution might suddenly material-ize; Bett was now willing to expect the most remote possibility. And so he made them wait.

Adam took in a deep breath, hunched his shoulders, and smiled just a little. How calming was his smile, how Bett liked him. "Jeremy," he said, "I think Eugene and I should talk alone for a bit. You've done a great job."

Jeremy gathered up his papers and pulled on his suede coat, and Bett and Adam watched him walk to the front of the café to disappear into the whiteness beyond the door. "E. G. was right," Adam said. "She knew you wouldn't be willing to commit to a sum like that without knowing anything about the play, without being sure we could pull it off. Businessmen are cautious. I understand that, Eugene, I even appreciate it in a way. That's why I can make one other proposal. Do you want to hear it?"

"Yes, I do," Bett said.

"It goes like this. You make an initial investment so that we can begin rehearsals. Support us for the first two weeks. We'll put a reserve on the theatre and pay out what-ever else can't wait. You can observe our rehearsals — we'll work every night and on the weekends so that people can continue their day jobs. At the end of two weeks we'll present an initial performance for you, not even a dress rehearsal but something that will show you what the play can be. What it *will* be. The only reason we're willing to do this, Eugene, is because we know we can win you over. There isn't one of us in the last year who hasn't broken down and wept, who hasn't crossed that last barrier. We think we can get you to cross it too. We're ready for this play, we'll peak with it and give the audience an experience they don't even know they could have. We've got to do it, Eugene. We need you."

Bett played with his cup in its saucer. "May I ask how much this initial investment would be?"

"Five thousand dollars."

"I'm not sure the arrangement would work. The company might resent my — my hesitation. I do not think I could attend rehearsals in that atmosphere."

"They won't know. E.G. and I will tell them that you're giving the full support."

"Would that be right?"

"It's the only way to get their total motivation. They're my actors, I can take care of them."

"Yes," Bett said. He reached into his jacket and from the inside pocket drew out a single cheque, folded in half. He laid it on the table and, taking Adam's proffered pen, slowly filled it in. "I make no promises after two weeks," Bett said.

"It isn't necessary." Adam's voice shook. "You'll see, you'll just see."

⚬⚬

Resting on the stone bench, facing the arch, which was a dirtier white than the snow swirling over the ground, Bett might have been taken for a statue, or a coat wrapped around a snowman. The cold made his nose and toes tingle, as if they were asserting their existence, and even Bett's phantom arm signalled its presence. Its "ache" had faded decades ago, but now it seemed to be coming back, as if the limb were regenerating itself. He was half-convinced that he could take his real hand from his pocket and give this other a confirming pat.

The night before, he had gone to bed, drained from the meeting with Adam and Jeremy. Not until he rose out of his slippers and tucked his feet into the bed had he realized how exhausting the silence had been. But in the morning he had awoken eager to rise. He had snapped on the radio, laid out his breakfast, hummed as he bustled about. All those Sundays he had spent in cold chapels, the solitary walks he had taken in the hope of even a brief conversation with a stranger — all of that seemed as distant as his life before America. Now there were young people happy to make him one of their own, and thirty thousand dollars did not seem so unreasonable a price. He did wonder, though, at their assumption of his wealth; for all their beautiful brightness they had failed to see anything. Yet they were right to feel sure of their own specialness, and he found himself believing what he once would have dismissed: that some real angel would materialize to grant them all their wishes.

The snow had started to fall again, making ghosts of the surrounding apartment houses. A form emerged onto the square — a dog or a child, he couldn't tell which. Either one was a good sign, although he wondered why it should be alone. He himself was not alone, not really; he was merely away from his friends for a time. He felt both pity for and superior to whatever it was and he rose from the bench, just as the form disappeared behind the arch. Standing there, looking down at his overcoat, which had turned white, he considered whether he might in fact *be* an angel, and Adam and Jessica and the others were the purpose for his being here. It was a ridiculous idea, but wonderful, he thought even as he waved it from his mind.

The keys jangled in his hand, all the way up the elevator and along the hallway to his own door. This afternoon he was glad to retire to his own rooms, to thaw himself out over a cup of hot tea and then perhaps lie down for a nap. He had been sleeping well lately, as deeply as a young man. As neither Adam nor any of the others had thought to ask him where he lived, they had defined his apartment as a kind of sanctuary, giving it a new meaning. So he was mildly disappointed to hear the door opening behind him and to turn and see Miss Drew in a terrycloth robe, an elasticized band holding her hair back from her face. Miss Drew appeared to have a cold, for her nose was a dull red, her eyes watery, and she held a box of tissues in her hand.

"I thought so," she said, sounding to Bett like *I tod zo*. "I mean, who else would it be?" and she gave one of her abrupt laughs. "Come in and have some tea, that is if you don't mind being with an ugly, sick person."

"Perhaps you'd prefer to rest by yourself," Bett said even as he followed her into an apartment shrouded by curtains and moist from a steamer hissing by the bedroom door. "I'm sick of resting," she said. "This is my third cold this winter. I must have low resistance or something. Turn up the TV if you want, I'll just nip into the kitchen. It's a detective movie. You can tell me what I miss."

Bett hung his overcoat in the hall and sat down on the edge of the sofa. "You're sure coming and going at all hours," Miss Drew called from the kitchen. "What's going on? You delivering drugs for the Mafia or something?" Bett managed a chuckle, and was tempted to tell her about the Genesis Theatre Company. What a thrill it would be to speak casually about them to somebody else, but Miss Drew might not appreciate the change in his status — she who preferred to see him as one of her own kind. But when she came in with the tea tray he was at least determined to change the tone of their tête-à-têtes.

"Miss Drew," he said cheerfully, "do you not think the new snow falling on the streets is pretty? I cannot recall such a late spring."

"Pretty? Are you out of your mind? Between here and the subway I almost got frostbite. A taxi driver sprayed slush over my good coat — I swear he did it on purpose. And what about those men standing around the trash-can fire at the corner? Making their remarks, I'm not afraid to tell them where to get off. Oh sure, it's as pretty as a picture on the bank calendar."

Bett sipped his tea, subdued but still determined to resist Miss Drew's litany of complaints. Of course she had suffered a terrible loss, but life went on and a person only saw the bad things if he looked for them. It was clear that Miss Drew did not want to be happy.

"Isn't there anything in the city that you like?" he asked.

"Not really," she sniffed and broke a cookie in two.

"Nothing at all? Some little thing?"

She gave him a look. "I like the fact that they passed the poop-and-scoop law."

"Really, Miss Drew, nothing else?"

"No. Are you deaf?" She raised a half-cookie from a long dunk in the tea cup, rushing it to her mouth before it fell apart. "Well," she said, searching the corner of her mouth with her tongue for crumbs, "something when I was a kid. We used to come into the city at Christmas to see the lights and we'd bring our skates. The whole family would go down to Central Park in the late afternoon and skate on the rink. My brother was a good skater and he taught me how to skate backwards. When it got dark they'd turn on the lights in the trees and we'd keep going round and round, until we got pains in our ankles. Afterwards we'd go to Howard Johnson's for hot chocolate and I'd be so tired that I'd fall asleep in the booth."

"Perhaps they have skating still," Bett said.

"Who knows. Drug pushers and gangs on skates. Not my idea of fun."

"When I was a child we also went skating," Bett said. He had forgotten that.

"Did I eat all those cookies myself?" Miss Drew laughed. "What a pig!"


<u>V</u>


The nine members of the company and Bett sat in a circle on the wooden floor of the studio, cross-legged or with knees up, close enough so that their arms touched.

Adam Frutkin smiled, looked down at the floor, rubbed his chin, and looked up again.

"We've been working together a long time, almost a year," he said quietly. "We've gone through a lot. We've learned to trust and understand each other. And to believe in the need that all of us have for the theatre. Remember, Vincent, how you resisted those Grotowski exercises?"

"I was scared," Vincent said. "But everybody helped me."

"We've all had those moments. Resisting the next step forward. And we've all needed help. You could say that we've worked through the whole history of modern theatre, a century of innovation and struggle in less than a year. And now we're here. Naturally we've all been anxious to go beyond exercises and workshops and scene studies, to a real production. But we've held off, or rather E.G. and I have. We didn't think that we were ready, any of us. And now we are. I don't mean that we know everything now, that there's nothing more to learn. But we're ready. It's time to show others what we can do."

Adam uncrossed his legs and pulled one knee to his chest. "In retrospect I see that E.G. and I always knew what kind of play we wanted to do. But we resisted it for a long while, just the way that all of us resist that next step up because it looks more precarious than the last. To go forward, we realized, we have to go all the way back. To Aeschylus. Sophocles. Euripides. The Greek playwrights. What draws us to them, why after some two and a half thousand years do they still have that power? E.G. and I tried to ignore that magnetism, we thought we wanted a play that was brand new, the latest, the cutting edge. But we kept coming back to those Greek plays. Their honesty. The beauty of their language. The compelling force of their stories. In the middle of the night I would find lines suddenly sounding in my head. Like this one: "From the gods who sit in grandeur, grace comes somehow violent." That's beautiful, isn't it? But also terrifying."

Adam paused again. He put his hands together and touched them to his lips. "It's a paradox," he said, "but sometimes to do something new you have to follow tradition. Probably every great modern theatre company has turned to a Greek play to prove itself, like a rite of passage. For us to do so is to be part of a ritual, and E.G. has helped us to understand the meaning of rituals."

Adam looked at E.G. across the circle. She was holding her wire glasses in her hands and now she slipped them on. "For a long time I've wondered what it was about the community of Greece that allowed the playwrights to speak so directly to it. Those plays have a richness and a substance that no writer seems to be able to create anymore. But at the same time we simply can't become part of that tradition. We can no longer make the same assumptions because the values they're based on have become so tarnished. The Greek plays give meaning and value through pattern. The repetition of action that moves inexorably towards fate. But in our world we know that pattern doesn't give meaning anymore. Oh, we have lots of patterns, lots of contemporary ritual. But now it does the opposite: it breeds meaninglessness. Now pattern just gives more pattern, in a mockery of value. That's the world we live in and that's the ground we have to work. To give the audience the tradition and at the same time to show that the tradition has become a lie."

"The Greek plays operate on a certain constant idea," said Adam. "Tragic determinism, that's what E.G. calls it. As if the universe had some fierce mechanism running it, moving the story towards its inevitable moment of blood and revelation. The tragedy is bound to happen, it leads to further horror — but eventually it comes to rest. We're just thankful that the gods have chosen somebody else for suffering. We feel exhausted and at peace. No doubt the Greek audience went home from the amphitheatre elated, whistling their way down the street. The demons were exorcised and the world was safe again. But *we* know differently. The world isn't safe anymore. A single day in our city is worse than a hundred years of Greek history. The Greeks could never have imagined the brutalities that now make the evening news. Watching it is the remnant of a ritual that has lost all meaning. We've seen too much of it, and instead of giving us peace it leaves us frightened and bored. There's no redemption, there's just more and more."

A low rumble of traffic rose from Canal Street. Adam reached behind and pulled from his pocket a rolled-up manuscript that he tossed into the circle. The actors stared at it, trying to read the single word typed on the first white page. "This is our play," he said. "We're going to make new from the old. Like alchemy. Which play is it, E.G.?"

"It's all of them," E.G. said. "Aeschylus, Sophocles, Euripides. *The Oresteia*, the Oedipus trilogy, *Electra*, *The Trojan Women, Medea*. You might say that we're stealing the best from them all. We could never use just one, because each is too coherent. Maybe there was a time when the people, the whole city could speak in one voice, like the chorus. But that was so long ago we can't see it from here, or we can see it only by looking backwards, in a cracked mirror. We're making the Greek plays modern by shattering the tradition. We've got no choice."

"Here's another way of putting it," Adam said. "Imagine that one night you turn on the television and by some amazing coincidence there's a Greek play on every channel. You have your remote control in your hand and *zap*, from *Agamemnon* to *Women of Trachis* to *Medea*. At first you're amazed by the coincidence, it's incredible, but then as you watch you become appalled by each play, by the emotion and the agony, and you switch faster and faster, trying to find a way out. That's our play. Is there a way out? Can we pull from it something genuine, some new heart of meaning? This won't be easy, not for us or for the audience. And if it sounds scary, well, it's scary to us too. But we're not here to do the easy thing. Everything is crazy and impossible and we do it, right?" He clapped his hands. "Okay, let's get started."

&#8471;

The third rehearsal did not end until after midnight, when the company declared itself "starving" and swept up the street to Tiffany's on Sheridan Square. Bett could hardly believe that the actors had the strength to eat after such an exhausting session; he himself was wrung out merely from watching. But the thought of food renewed them and they carried Bett along, Jessica holding his arm and the rest crowding about and noisy, as if affectionately leading the team mascot. They streamed into the diner, voices rising, and began shifting tables together, only to sit down and jump up again, as if playing musical chairs. When the waiter came over, they vigorously debated the menu and shouted their orders: burgers, onion rings, milkshakes.

Bett tried to order tea but Jessica wouldn't let him and he conceded to a chocolate sundae. The diner was not so different from the one he frequented, with its overly bright lighting and plastic domes over the cream pies on the counter. But the company transformed it. The noise grew until other diners turned to stare, but the attention only made them more outrageous. One end of the table played a game with spoons and glasses while the other debated British and American acting styles. And, in the middle, Vincent was being urged to perform his infamous imitation of a certain Hollywood star; the star was Vincent's uncle but wouldn't make so much as a phone call to help his nephew's career.

When the food arrived (on enormous trays carried by two waiters), the company began to praise its "presentation" in French accents. But their table manners were decidedly American. They spoke with mouths brimming, they poured ketchup on their plates. Bett looked at Jessica, who was laughing as Adam spoke, his mouth near her ear. She was the most alive of them all, and he appreciated simply being able to watch her. When she caught him looking she narrowed her eyes and smiled just slightly, a private message for him.

On the other side of Bett, Miriam lit a cigarette as she talked. She always looked tired, which Bett realized had its own allurement, and he missed her first words while admiring the skill with which she flared her nostrils to expel jets of smoke. ". . . And if I'm right, then modern techniques taken too far can be self-defeating. What I'm trying to show Adam is the fallacy of imitation. To express alienation you don't want to actually alienate the audience from the play. You're just perpetuating the condition, do you see?"

"An interesting point," Bett said. "Then alienation is what the company — what we want to express?"

"What I'm trying to do is get Adam to see the legitimacy of melodrama, not as mere emotion, but as method. Of course I never got to see any of the genuine melodramas, but I've read the accounts of early immigrant theatre. For them, ambiguity counted for nothing. Their audience wanted to cry, and I mean floods of tears. Talk about breaking the fourth wall! They wept, shouted, demanded. They didn't expect to pay their money and then sit with their mouths shut. Who cared about respectability! You know who understood this? Kafka! He loved Yiddish actors. We've got to bring the life-blood back to the theatre."

Miriam lit another cigarette, not with a disposable lighter, but one of ornate silver. "You seem to know a good deal about it," Bett said, "Do you think Adam will listen?"

"Oh, Adam always listens. He takes in everything. I know he's going to be a major cultural figure. And look at E.G., in the midst of this craziness she's underlining in some French journal. Sometimes I think I should have been born two or three generations ago. I would have liked to have been an actress in Jacob Adler's company and played the good daughter in *The Jewish King Lear*. All those tired faces in the audience gazing up at me, stricken, moved to tears. I would have loved it."

A bright flash made them look up. Adrian stood on a chair, holding a camera. "Miriam," he squinted through the viewfinder, "tell Eugene about the part you just got in the new Chevy Chase picture. Miriam's a star."

"I've got three lines," she laughed up smoke as the camera flashed again. "And I get to throw a Cuisinart out a window."

ↂ

During rehearsals, Bett's place was a folding chair against the long wall of the studio, where he would sit without moving from the opening movement exercises to the final winding down. Rehearsal, Adam said, was a holistic process, a spiral, requiring an order and rhythm to take the actors "out" of the world and then place them back again. Bett watched with a wonder undiminished by his inability to decipher the meaning or even the point of what he saw. There was no reading aloud of the script or walking through the actions as he had expected. Only after a few days could he begin to see how Adam worked round and back again to the play, and scenes began to emerge, if only in fragments. From his chair, Bett felt as if he were participating in the rehearsal, and he sometimes caught himself tensing his own body in imitation, or making soundless words with his tongue. At other times he became drowsy and nodded off to sleep. On the first of these occasions he awoke to confusion and embarrassment, but soon he found these naps natural and even pleasant, and upon awakening he more than once saw one of the members of the company gazing at him as if he were a newborn baby.

On the fourth day of rehearsal a row of photographs appeared on the wall behind Bett's chair. They were pinned at the corners, four of them with colours so washed out they looked hand-tinted, like photographs he remembered from childhood. Bett stood and stared at them for some moments before recognizing the scene as Tiffany's: Adam with a hamburger in his mouth, E. G. peering over the top of her journal, even Bett staring at his sundae, each with a blurry background of faces and hands. He could not recall the last time anyone had taken his picture and wasn't sure if he cared to be so recorded, not when there were no such documents of his other past, all trace of which was lost. But like it or not, there he was up on the wall. In truth, he was a little surprised that he could be photographed at all, as if there ought to have been only an empty chair and a hovering spoon. He was sallow-faced but real, with half of Jessica next to him, her hand touching his sleeve. Perhaps it was her touch that made him real; a moment earlier he would not have been there.

At the next day's rehearsal a second row of photographs appeared beside the first. These had been taken during rehearsal and Bett had the strange sensation, when turning from the wall to the studio, of the photographs appearing real and the ongoing rehearsal an image in a frame. In the next day's row, at the bottom, so that Bett had to stoop slightly to see it, was a different sort of photograph. A portrait of Jessica. She stood alone in the studio, looking at the camera and without any clothes on — just a wooden bracelet on one wrist. She was as thin as a girl who had grown too fast, her arms dangling at her sides. Looking at it, Bett felt his heart skip, and it took several seconds for him to understand that nobody had done this to Jessica, that she wanted to make herself this vulnerable.

Bett could not look at the real Jessica for the rest of the rehearsal.

The day after, another portrait appeared in the new row, this one of a naked Jeremy, kneeling on the studio floor, his head tilted back as if he were a sacrifice. It had the effect of making Jessica at least appear less prominent. The following day Annette joined their ranks, her back to the camera and her arms stretched across one of the dark windows. Bett was examining this addition when Vincent came up beside him. Adam was working with three actors on the space marked on the floor with red tape to duplicate the dimensions of the theatre's stage.

"Adrian calls this the documentary wall," Vincent said. "After the show's a hit he's going to publish them in a book."

"A book? But would everyone like that?"

"Sure, who wouldn't?"

"Well, Annette for one. There she is without any clothes."

"He's taking all of us like that so it's all right." And then Vincent half-whispered her name. And again, "Annette."

"Are you fond of her?"

"Fond! I love her, that's all. I have for six months."

"Perhaps you should tell her."

"Oh, she knows."

"She does?"

"Sure, we talk about it all the time. For hours. You know what she says? She's *sorry* for me. I hate that. She wants to love me, she says she would if she could, but she can't. She's crazy about Jeremy."

"Jeremy?"

"She doesn't even love him, she admits that. She's *infatuated*. Of course Jeremy's gay so it's pretty futile. They tried two or three times, but it didn't work, not after the first time."

"Annette told you this?"

"They both did. She hates it when I plead. She says I'm always looking at her —"

A crash made them turn. Bett looked at the still tableau of actors: Ramona, Adrian, and Jessica, and Adam standing before them. Then the tableau melted and Jessica started to cry. "How can I?" she asked, her face and hands trembling. Ramona took a step towards her but looked at Adam and stopped. Adam merely crossed his arms.

E. G. drifted to Bett's side, holding a rolled-up script in her hand. "They're scared," she whispered. "They're afraid of not having enough to hold on to. It's what we've taken out — they keep losing themselves."

"Are you going to make changes?" Bett asked.

"What for? It's going better than we dreamed."

Bett awoke in the middle of the night. He was standing in his nightshirt by the open bedroom window, snow drifting in from the sill. For the third night in a row, faces only half-recognized came to him, speaking close to his ear. Tonight one had called him away, a woman, her features already fading. She had had red hair, narrow eyes, thin arms. He was shivering; he closed the window and went back to bed.

∽

On the evening of the last rehearsal, Bett agreed to meet Jessica at the Strand Book Store. He wasn't sure why she had asked him, but he eagerly walked the few blocks to Broadway so that he arrived several minutes early. Inside, people searched through bins of discounted books, keeping their coats buttoned up as the store was as cold as a warehouse, which it resembled. Bett looked idly and without concentration, gazing up every few moments in the hope of seeing Jessica. It was foolish, but waiting, he felt like a boy again. What he wanted now was merely to know her, to be allowed to care about her and to watch her charmed life from a distance. This did not seem a lot to ask, yet it was infinitely more than he dared even desire just weeks ago.

He hadn't seen Jessica come in, but there she was three rows away, frowning as she sorted through a bin of books. She wore a man's big overcoat (it had been left behind in her apartment, she had told him; all her clothes seemed to have belonged to other people) and a square hat on her head, her hair tied back. She saw him too and they met half way.

"I'm looking for a book for you," she said. "But I can't find it. It has a green cover."

"Ah, a green cover. I believe that is in the gardening section."

"Very funny! This isn't a joking matter, Eugene. I think this book would be very good for you. Oh look, isn't that amazing? Here it is, in the bin right beside you."

"Like it was waiting for us," he chuckled as she picked it up. Could it really be the book that she was looking for, or was she pretending? It was small and plain and inside, he saw as she opened it, were just a few sentences on each page, cheerful and vaguely mystical aphorisms.

"Go ahead, be sceptical," she said. "But I'm going to buy it for you and then you'll see. Sometimes a book can change your life. We better hurry or we'll be late for the rehearsal."

She gave it to him to hold while she paid at the cashier. Outside, he slipped it into his coat pocket as they walked, she holding onto his arm. "You have a spiritual temperament," he said.

"What a nice way of putting it. I guess so. I mean, I've always felt there was something else other than just us. Or maybe something else that is also us. But I don't believe in any one thing, there's no reason to limit the possibilities. Spirits, souls, gods, worlds. If you can imagine something then it must be true, don't you think? It's like the way that E.G. and the others worry about me walking home by myself after rehearsals. They're sweet to think of me, but I know that nothing bad will ever happen. It's a matter of believing. That probably sounds simple-minded, but I guess faith always does when you're outside it. I don't want anybody to worry about me — that's too much negativity. I want them to know everything will always be all right. I want you to know that, Eugene."

"Me?"

"Especially you."

When they arrived the rehearsal was just starting. Bett receded to his customary chair. Every day another row of photographs had been pinned to the documentary wall, a gallery of hands in movement and intense faces in close-up. The tradition of the naked portrait had also continued and, in spite of himself, Bett anticipated each new day's addition. Here now was E. G., sitting in one of the folding chairs, her feet planted on the ground and her elbows on her knees, staring brazenly. Only Adam was left to be photographed, unless Adrian was planning to include Bett in his documentary project. Bett had seen Adrian look at him as if trying to work up his courage to ask. How grotesque that would be, a photograph of an old man with one arm next to those young and flawless bodies. But what if Adrian did ask? Bett was afraid that he might begin to strip then and there, discarding his jacket and tie in a heap on the floor.

Tomorrow evening the company would perform their play for an audience of one. Sitting in his chair, Bett could no longer put off thinking about the final commitment he was expected to make when it was over. The pain he felt at having to disappoint them was hardly relieved by a growing conviction that what he saw taking shape within the red tape markings on the floor he never could have agreed to.

Not that the play he finally saw emerging was bad;

he was incapable of judging whether it was laughable or brilliant. He knew only that he could not bear to watch the actors go through their roles. Jeremy and Adrian and Ramona and Vincent and Miriam and Annette and Jessica — each took several parts and in these last days of rehearsal they seemed to sink deeper inside their characters, as if merging them with their own selves. It apparently began with Iphigenia, Agamemnon's daughter, kneeling to be sacrificed so that the Athenian ships could sail for Troy. Then Jocasta hung herself and Oedipus gouged out his eyes. In quick succession came the murders of Cassandra and Laius, followed by the lingering death by poison of Heracles. As one scene dissolved into another the actors in front faded back and those behind moved up. Eurydice killed herself with a sword; Antigone by a rope. Orestes killed his mother in revenge, Medea slaughtered her children in jealousy. Between each death was acted fragments of the original plays, or else the chorus (all those not in the scene unfolding) chanted out lines, sometimes like a dirge and sometimes in a frenzy. Phaedra hung herself — for shame of love, the chorus said — while Theseus walked about with his mangled and dying son in his arms. Polynices was buried, dug up, buried again, and pulled up rotting to be torn apart by actors turned into dogs.

Atreus ate the flesh of his own children.

Deineria spread her husband's bedclothes out and kneeling on them ran her sword into her stomach.

Orestes went mad. Ajax went mad. The play ended.

❦

E.G. stood near a window of the studio, beneath a single illuminated bulb, the last left on after the rest of the company had gone. Bett stood by a pillar, in half-shadow; he cleared his throat. She had asked him to stay behind, but the others had left several minutes ago and still she remained silent. In her presence he felt himself shrink and waver, like a mirage.

"My father owns this building," she said, half turning in the light. "He gives us the space rent-free. He owns several others in the city."

"I would never have known," Bett said.

"Because I don't show I come from money? That's funny, Adam says it's written all over me. We're going to have to vacate soon, the building's being turned into what they call a 'media centre' — advertising firms, recording studios. Adam wanted me to tell you that tomorrow night, before you arrive for the performance, we're going to tell the company that you haven't committed to the play."

"Why would you do that?"

"We both agree that it's wrong to keep it a secret any longer. It would be dishonest. And besides, it's no longer useful. Adam thinks they'll give their best if they know what they're fighting for."

"I see."

"Are you uncomfortable with that?"

"I have no reason to be. It's the truth."

"Of course, if you decide to support us it won't make any difference. Adam's convinced that you will. Have you already made your decision, Eugene?"

"Why do you ask that?"

"Just a hunch. Well, don't answer. I can wait until tomorrow. If you decide in our favour that's great. If you decide the other way — well, that's an interesting situation too."

"Forgive me," Bett said, and taking a handkerchief from his pocket he wiped his forehead. "But I don't understand you. May I ask a question?"

"Please."

"Your father is obviously a wealthy man. If I should choose not to finance the show, couldn't he be your angel? Perhaps for tax purposes —"

"Nope," she shook her head. "I wouldn't even ask. That's not my contribution to this company. It's getting late. Tomorrow's a big day."

"Yes. May I escort you to your door?"

"It isn't necessary. I always take a cab." She pulled the cord of the light.

## VI

Bett knotted his tie before the spotted mirror and then turned a little to the side to judge its appearance. He had spent a full hour picking it out that morning; after all, the first new tie in years, and for a special occasion, could not be treated lightly The tie proved that he approached the evening's performance with the proper attitude — not with dread, as he had increasingly felt the last few days, but with a sense of expectation and style. After all, he had never promised anything to the company more than he had given.

And when he thought about it, was it not he himself who had been used in some way? Their friendship, their hugs and kisses came eagerly while he was paying the bills. But once they knew that he would pay no more? No doubt they would turn their backs upon him. Even Jessica? Yes, even Jessica.

Bett adjusted the flattened sleeve at his side and then slipped on his overcoat. He had spent the day in a return to his routine of only a few weeks ago, knowing that after tonight he must go back to his old life. At the library he had smiled for Mrs Washington and settled down at the reading table where the other regulars raised their eyebrows at him, as if to say, "So you've decided to come back, have you?" As a slight deviation he had taken afternoon tea at the diner on Waverly Place; was he not, after all, a free man who could alter his day as he wished? To his surprise, he could still enjoy the taste of bread pudding. And afterwards, the afternoon in the park, where nannies with their strollers had been drawn by more pleasant weather, and he had made faces at a baby. Today, at last, Bett could feel summer approaching, when he would spend less time in his apartment and more outside, observing the vibrant life of the city like some municipal census-taker neutrally noting down facts.

The only dark spot this evening was the memory of a dream from the night before. How strange to have so many dreams lately, after years of blank spaces of sleep. In this one he saw himself sitting in the front row of a crowded and glittering Victorian theatre, a velvet palace with rotund balconies and plaster angels on the ceiling. The performance had just ended, but the audience, instead of applauding, filed silently down the aisles, leaving only Bett in his seat. The curtain rose again and there the company stood, holding hands, smiling in anticipation. As in the other dreams, their faces were familiar, intimate, yet he could not place them. Bett was so touched, so moved by the performance that he could not even raise his hand. The company looked about the empty theatre in astonishment and, seeing Bett, began to call down accusations upon him. They shouted with increasing fury and someone picked up a prop from the stage, a vase or an ashtray, and hurled it at him. The object hit his shoulder. More props were thrown, books, plates, a chair — all at Bett, who did not move, as if he deserved to be punished. They climbed down from the stage, shaking their fists, cursing . . .

Bett gave a final pull at the knot in his tie before opening the door. He could see, as if in a mirror, the door opposite his own opening too. The last person he wished to see this night was Miss Drew (he had decided not to make her part of his new routine), and he considered closing his own door quickly again. But even now good manners prevented him, and he came out smiling, as if the coincidence of finding Miss Drew in her doorway were the greatest luck.

"How delightful," Bett said, touching his imaginary brim. He saw that she had on her coat and was holding a box in her hands.

"I want to show you what I bought," she said, nudging off the lid of the box.

Bett employed his most apologetic tone. "I'm sorry, but

people are expecting me. Perhaps another time —"

"But it was because of you!" And balancing the box on one hand she lifted out a pair of figure skates. They were a pristine white and tied at the laces. "There is skating in Central Park. I checked. I was thinking we might go together. You can rent skates there and it's open late."

"My goodness, Miss Drew, I wouldn't remember how."

"You never forget, and besides I can show you. It would be fun."

"Yes, it would be. Let's certainly make a date, perhaps next week —"

"I'm too excited to wait. I went specially to Blooming-dale's on my lunch hour to buy them. Please."

The skates twirled from their laces, the blades glinting in the dim light. "Perhaps tonight you could find another friend," Bett said. "Or go by yourself."

"By myself? That isn't any fun."

But Bett was already taking a step down the hall. "Next week, Miss Drew!" Rather than wait for the elevator he skipped down the stairs and into the street. From the piles of blackened snow, rivulets flowed like little rivers on a map. Striding ahead, Bett felt a sudden confidence that everything would work out, that Adam and E.G. and Jessica — that the whole company would somehow find the happiness they desired. He felt ashamed to have thought even for a moment that the company had used him, when they had shown him the greatest affection he had known in years. Now he wanted to return it to them tenfold. He felt crazily like a young man off to persuade the parents of the girl he loves that they may entrust her to his care. He whistled his way down the sidewalk, nodding at the people already occupying tables outside the cafés. He paused only at a corner shop to buy a small bouquet of roses. By the time he reached Canal Street his shoes might have been gliding above the ground.

Outside the metal door of the studio, Bett was surprised to hear voices from inside. He had expected a hushed welcome and a quick ushering to his folding chair in the darkened space. The door opened and he saw a knot of company members, all speaking at once. When Adam saw Bett he pushed his way forward.

"Jesus, Eugene, you're here," Adam said. "Jessica hasn't shown up yet."

"I don't understand," Bett said.

"She was supposed to get here an hour and a half ago. Something must be wrong. Why are we all just standing here?"

E.G. came up to them. "Eugene," she said. "At first we thought Jessica was just late. But Jeremy went to her apartment and she wasn't there. Her door was open."

Just then Ramona and Vincent ran in through the doorway. "We talked to the police," Ramona gasped. "But they said it was too early for them to do anything."

"I can't stay here any longer," Miriam said. "I'm going out to look for her."

"I'll go with you," said Jeremy.

"Then let's all look," E.G. said. "I'm sure there's some silly explanation and after we find her we can all have a good cry. We better split up. I'll try our regular spots. Who knows where else she might hang out?"

The company tumbled into the street, sweeping Bett along. Then they scattered, leaving him with his bouquet of roses. Dusk was turning to night as he started back along the streets he had come, past shop windows that glowed dully. He understood that the performance would not go on because the others had gone to look for Jessica. *Because Jessica is missing.* He said that over and over to himself as he walked, unable to penetrate its meaning.

In the fish–bowl–shaped foyer of his building, Bett saw that something had changed. After a moment he realized that the furniture had been removed, even the armchairs with the long rips up their backs. Perhaps Miss Drew was still in her apartment; would it be too late to go skating? He passed the elevator and climbed the stairs, so that he was out of breath by the fourth floor. As he came down the hall, panting a little and clutching the bouquet to his chest, he saw that Miss Drew's door was open.

"Hello?" he called. He peered into the living room and saw bright colours flashing on the television screen. He stepped inside. On the table was the square box, with just one skate nestled among the tissue papers. The room was as neat as always, a pot of tea resting on the tray. He searched the kitchen, the bedroom, and the bathroom, and when he returned to the living room he saw that the window blind had been raised and the window hauled up as high as it could go. The iron gate to the fire escape had been unlocked and pushed aside. Gingerly he put his head out the window, but in the darkness he could see only the shadowy bars and lights across the street. "Miss Drew?" he called and, trying not to damage the bouquet as he tucked it under his arm, he pulled himself onto the fire escape.

He could see the water tanks on the apartments across. Ducking the safety bar, he stood up on the edge of the escape, groping for the bar behind him with his hand. A rose fell. Somewhere down there was Jessica. And not only her, but Miss Drew. Who was it that Jessica looked like from long ago? And Miss Drew, and Adam, and E. G., and the others? Yes, he remembered now; the bouquet unravelled into the air. All the faces of the dead came back to him at last. He had never forgotten! And this time he would keep them from harm. Over the city he stretched out his arms — both of them! — and for the first time became the real Eugene Bett, deserving of love.

# History Lessons

$\mathcal{T}$he wedding portrait of my mother and father that I possess is the one that my brother and I had framed for them years ago. Ronny was twenty-one and I was thirteen and we had just moved into the new house a month before. We thought it would make a nice anniversary gift — probably it was my idea, Ronny wasn't the sort to notice the absence of a wedding portrait displayed anywhere in the house. When our parents unwrapped the gift they made the appropriate sounds and even put the portrait on the mantel over the living-room fireplace for a while. One day, home from school, I noticed it was gone. I went searching for it and, sure enough, found it in the basement, back in the box of old photographs. Ronny, I don't think, ever noticed.

Months later, the new house didn't feel so strange to me and yet we still, as a family, didn't know how to fill it. My room, bare when I first slept there, now had prints of

English sailing ships on the walls and my aquarium, dismantled in the old house and the fish put in plastic bags, was set up again opposite the foot of my bed. But the house still had empty places in need of armchairs or sofas or bookcases to give them a meaning. It wasn't that my parents couldn't afford the furniture for the house they had arranged to be built, but that they were cautious. An interior decorator, whom I knew only as Dell, was assisting them in the piece-by-piece creation of the house they had always dreamed of. Persian carpets and Chinese blue-and-white porcelain, Quebec washstands and Louis the something-or-other chairs with spindly legs. All of these things had once belonged in other people's homes — that, I understood, was what was meant by antiques. In ours they seemed like museum pieces, the kind found in those houses my parents so loved to tour where velvet ropes prevented one from sitting in chairs. That they were lovely objects I could see even at the age of thirteen, having inherited some of my mother's natural taste. But we couldn't make the house ours. Instead, perhaps because my parents had wanted for too long, we seemed like caretakers. How lovingly they had planned the house, with a French-born architect who was bald and wore round glasses and drew on his cigar as he listened to my parents' hesitant suggestions. Then it was raised on the suburban lot, brick by blessed brick, as if it were to be the future family trust, passed on from one generation to another like estates in Jane Austen novels. In reality my parents would sell the house only ten years later, when the children were grown, and return to a house as small as the one they had started in.

This second June in the new house a late summer had finally arrived, I would turn fourteen in July, and in a week-and-a-half school would end and the summer holidays begin. I hated my new school, J.R. Henry Junior High, but even so I didn't want the year to end. If I could have believed that praying might by some miracle keep us in the classroom through the sweltering months of July and August I would have. But that was one prayer those desultory Sunday Hebrew classes, which I was allowed to give up after my Bar Mitzvah, hadn't taught me.

Last summer hadn't been so bad. Ronny and I had spent it splashing about in our new swimming pool beneath the rear balcony of the house. The pool was a simple rectangle, clear and blue, with a flagstone patio and deck chairs where my father took to sitting after work in a terrycloth robe with his evening paper. Ronny and I invented a half dozen water games. One favourite called for each of us in turn to push off the deep end while standing on a foam surfboard. My mother banned that one; she guaranteed (she always "guaranteed" things) that we would split our heads on the side of the pool.

It was the best time I ever spent with Ronny, before or since. Together beneath the water our skin turned the colour of dark brass. We were eight years apart and in a sense each an only child, equally coddled. To me my older brother had always been magnificent, and that summer only made him more so. But in the fall Ronny entered law school at the University of Toronto and by the following June it felt as if I hadn't seen him since. If he wasn't at the library then he was studying behind the closed door of his bedroom. On Saturday nights, when we had once watched the hockey game together, Ronny now went to law-school parties and came home late, long after I had lost the battle of trying to stay awake, listening for him. Although I missed his company I didn't say anything because I wanted him to do well at school, and my mother, I knew, hoped that he would finally begin to take out girls. Whether he had begun I didn't know as we never talked about that sort of thing. Last summer we had been friends, almost equals. But once again I had become the younger brother, the kid.

And so I had been pretty much on my own for the year. There was the rest of my family, of course, my mother and father and my father's family — Aunt Ida and her third husband, Mosey, my bachelor uncle Norman, and my grandmother. My mother's parents were dead and her sister and brothers had moved to Vancouver and California, but we saw a lot of my father's family. As my father said, we were the only relatives they had. When they came over I usually hung around unless I was suffering from, as Aunt Ida called them, "one of Matthew's moods." That was when they would wonder aloud where the cheerful little boy they once knew had gone. I didn't remember myself like that at all, but then I didn't care. If I felt very bad I stayed in my room and listened to my mother's portable radio-recorder or put on a jacket, even in the coldest days of February, and trudged to the end of the garden where I could see, past the back yards and houses behind us, the upper windows of J. R. Henry Junior High School.

My school, the school that I hated, the school I didn't want to leave for the summer holidays. Looking at those upper windows was the closest I could get to the girl I loved, Andrea Rapkin. I had been in love with Andrea for nine and a half months.

"Matthew, sweetheart, what's so interesting, staring out the window like that?"

That was my Aunt Ida, my father's older sister. We'd all gone to the buffet lunch at the Park Hotel, as we did almost every Sunday, and had come back to spend the rest of the afternoon at home. If it hadn't been drizzling we might have gone for a walk, especially if any new houses were going up on the street (my family's favourite occupation was standing in front of half-built houses), but we stayed in the living room instead, and through the sliding glass doors I could feel the waves of coolness from the rain. The television was turned on — its changing colours were reflected in the doors — but the sound was off and we listened instead to my mother's latest record on the stereo built into the cabinet. The record was Dvorak's *Slavonic Dances* and my mother had resisted putting it on, saying that no one really wanted to hear it. I knew she didn't want to play it; the record was too new, she preferred to listen in private. But Aunt Ida had insisted and as soon as the needle had touched the record she had gone into raptures.

"So touching — it goes right to the heart. Mosey, did you ever hear such music?"

Mosey (I never called him uncle) was perched on the armchair by the fireplace and, as usual, reading our latest issue of *Time* magazine. He was dressed meticulously in a double-breasted blazer with brass buttons embossed with anchors, neatly creased trousers, and white shoes. The clothes accentuated his thinness and he had a set of false teeth that gently clacked when he spoke, a sound I liked. Perhaps because of his stutter Mosey didn't talk much and hours would go by when I forgot he was even in the room. Now, frowning at some article in the magazine, he said aloud, "This . . . this is q-quite outrageous . . . and t-to think . . ." and mumbled back into silence without anyone taking notice.

My grandmother sat on the end of the leather sofa that faced the flagstone wall, smiling a little, her stubby fingers entwined. Since last winter she had developed trouble with her balance and preferred to stay put. My grandmother didn't speak much either, although whether it was because she had little to say or felt such contempt for her family that she didn't wish to waste her breath I didn't know. Sometimes when I sat beside her on the sofa she would take my hand and hold it with surprising strength.

Next to the upright piano, which only Ronny could play and hadn't for months, stood my father and Uncle Norman, talking about some property in Burlington. Uncle Norman looked a lot like my father, only taller, with thinning hair and, unlike his accentless brother, an inability to pronounce the word "thick." From what I could follow, my uncle had forgotten about a tract of land he owned, and the city, after several years of non-payment of taxes, had taken it away. Uncle Norman, who still lived with my grandmother, seemed both ashamed and indifferent.

"You never change, Norman, not from day one. How could you —"

I stopped listening and turned to watch my mother

enter the room holding a crystal bowl of fruit. She took it around and Mosey, without rising from his chair, selected an orange. When I was young he had enjoyed amazing me by peeling an orange in a single unbroken spiral, but the trick's interest had worn off long ago and he no longer called to me, "S-see, Matthew, see, this is r-real talent."

Uncle Norman tapped a piano key and turned with relief to my mother. "What a sight, straight from the garden of Eden," he said, reaching for an apple. "You put those wealthy Rosedale matrons to shame."

"Really, Norman," my mother shooed him away.

"But it's true," he said, winking at me.

"Oh no, after such a lunch who can eat?" Aunt Ida protested. She swayed to Dvorak under a Calder lithograph of two yellow shapes that looked to me like bananas. My mother just gave my father one of her looks. Aunt Ida said, "Does it have to rain on the weekend? I want to get out, to move, to smell the air. A person needs to be outdoors —"

"Ida, have a plum," my mother said. "They're just ripe today."

Aunt Ida took the plum. "That flower arrangement in the hall is gorgeous," she said. "You have a natural artistic talent."

"It's simple, Ida. You put the flowers in a vase."

"No, I could see how you drooped the willow branch on one side and balanced it with the rose blooms. That's composition, I can spot it. You have a Japanese touch. Ma, did you see what I mean? Come take a look."

"I'll look later."

"You'll see I'm right." Aunt Ida bit into the plum. "My God, what a fruit! So sweet, so juicy. Mosey, try a plum, they're incredible."

A rivulet of juice travelled down Aunt Ida's chin. Mosey took a napkin from my mother and tucked it in his collar. She held the crystal bowl to him and he hesitated, examining one plum and then another. My mother looked frazzled; I imagined her hurling the bowl against the flagstone wall.

"Don't you have any grapes?" my grandmother said. "I like seedless."

Aunt Ida was forty-seven years old, although I wasn't supposed to know. One day she had left her pocketbook on the kitchen counter and I took a peek at her driver's licence. She wasn't young, but as my father liked to say, she put a lot of the kids to shame with her energy. Aunt Ida didn't like to keep still. She worked every day at a bridal shop downtown, although that was due to necessity. Every evening she went to the Jewish Y two blocks from their apartment on Bathurst Street, where she ran around the track, swam, played badminton. At night while Mosey slept she sat up in bed beside the lamp and read historical novels. She was an insomniac.

My father often said that Aunt Ida should get her real-estate licence. A natural saleswoman like her would make a killing, unlike her husband who had a breakfast meeting every morning but hadn't made a sale in years. "I'm not interested in dirtying my hands," she would always say. She couldn't be called pretty. She had a prominent nose like her brothers, heavy lips, and she plucked her eyebrows into arches. But she had what my father called a womanly figure, and whenever we met her for lunch on Bloor Street I saw men stare at her bosom. Her hair was reddish-brown, an unreal colour, but it helped her look younger, and she kept her blouse unbuttoned a little daringly. When she bent over, say to pour cream in her coffee, I could see a mole on the rounding curve of her left breast that would hypnotize me until I noticed my mother's stare of disapproval.

Uncle Norman called his sister a very hip woman and I guessed it was true. She owned copies of two Beatles albums. The bracelets on her wrist were bought from a man with long hair and earrings in Yorkville. On weekends she wore bellbottom slacks (my mother who was younger never would) and when my father read aloud from the paper about some new university protest in the United States she always sided with the students. She used expressions like "whatever turns you on" and sometimes she said, "I was born too early."

Mosey closed the magazine in his lap and looked up. He was, or so my parents said, just like Aunt Ida's first two husbands, practically a carbon copy. He had bundled the pit of the plum in a napkin and was considering where to put it down. "What, still raining? Still — that rain?"

"A philosopher," my grandmother snorted. She had passed on some resemblance to Aunt Ida — hazel eyes, heavy jowls, and a retreating chin that although not evident in my father had in turn been passed on to me. Her hair was coloured the same as her daughter's by the same hairdresser, only her scalp could be seen in places. She looked sourly at Mosey.

"A paper cut-out, that's what you are."

"It's going to rain all night," I said, brushing the bangs from my eyes. I felt sorry for Mosey and sometimes tried to distract my grandmother's attention. I wondered why she could be so mean; perhaps it was the only way of using up the energy left in her, her last signal of defiance. Mosey never spoke back to her; he pretended not to hear. I could see my own faint image in the glass door and I tried to study my face the way teenagers, I know now, often look in mirrors hoping to discover who they are. I wanted to know if what I felt — about Andrea Rapkin, that is — showed in my mouth, my eyes, as I thought it ought to, as I thought it must. But I couldn't tell. What I saw was an oval face that didn't even look its thirteen years.

On the other side of my reflection was the back garden and the pool, the plastic winter-cover heaped on the deck. On Sunday the classrooms of J.R. Henry would be deserted, the halls sprinkled with chemical-odorous shavings, but there was some comfort in knowing that tomorrow Andrea would be there. I must have been the only student at J.R. Henry who looked forward to Mondays.

"What's so fascinating, are you ever going to tell me?" Aunt Ida's voice was so near it made me start. "Turn around, your aunt wants a hug." I obeyed and, while the rest of the family watched the television screen, Aunt Ida put her arms around me. She made a murmuring sound against my ear and I felt the roundnesses of her breasts flatten against my chest.

"Was that the door?" my mother said. Aunt Ida let go. We turned towards the opening to the hall, which framed a sort of picture: the spiral of the bannister, dried flowers blossoming from an oriental vase, the lower tiers of the chandelier. And into that picture slid Ronny's grin that was so much like our father's, followed by the rest of him until he stood before us in his wet sneakers, holding his knapsack of books. Ronny squinted into the living room at us, the way he sometimes looked into my aquarium.

"Mr Lawyer," Uncle Norman said. "Long time no see. Hitting the books again, eh?"

Mosey's thin frame jerked out of his chair like a yanked marionette. "Ronny. Here, in *Time* magazine. A big law s-suit . . ."

"I ran home from the bus stop," Ronny panted. "That rain is fantastic."

"You should have called, we would have picked you up," my father said.

My mother stood up. "Go up and change and I'll make dinner."

"Already ate, our study group ordered pizza. Sorry, I have to go upstairs and work. Torts."

"Dessert then," my mother said.

"Sure, a little later. Hey, Matt."

"Yeah, Ronny?"

"Come up after. I've got something for you."

Then he swung upstairs and we all — my mother and father, Uncle Norman, Aunt Ida and Mosey, my grand-mother and I — watched him until his legs disappeared from view. He had only run home in the rain but I looked at him in wonder, as if he had crossed the Atlantic in a rowboat. My mother never let us walk in the rain — that

was how you caught pneumonia. It seemed to me that
Ronny lived a separate life from the rest of us now; that he
was, somehow, of the world.

"He looks skinny," Aunt Ida said.

"He's fine," said my mother. "Matthew, have you
finished your homework for tomorrow?"

My father's family stayed for dinner. They didn't ask to
stay, my mother didn't invite them. They just stayed. That's
what usually happened and when my mother announced
dinner and they filed into the kitchen and looked at the
steaming lasagna, they expressed surprise at the late hour and
insisted they would never think of staying. Then we all sat
down and ate.

During dinner the telephone rang and my father got
up to answer. It was Howard Klapperman, my best, really
my only, friend at school, wanting the answer to a math
question. I had already done my homework (my mother
knew that and I resented her even asking me) on Saturday
morning, done it adequately so as not to be called upon by
my teachers for either notable achievement or failure. But
I was naturally good in math and found it hard not to do
well. I always gave Howard the answers. I had to. He knew
my secret.

Back at the table Uncle Norman said, "Who was that,
one of your girlfriends?"

"Brigitte Bardot," I said. "She won't leave me alone."

After dinner I carried a wedge of sponge cake and a
glass of milk up the spiral staircase, careful not to spill.
Every two months my mother and Eugenia, our cleaning
lady, spent a day dusting the chandelier, my mother bracing

the ladder while Eugenia wiped each crystal teardrop with a rag. I thought of how Ronny's desk was weighted with legal tomes, while I still used books called *Pathways Through History* and *Ici on parle français*. For some reason I thought about the night last summer when I'd been allowed to stay up and watch Neil Armstrong step onto the dust of the moon, and Ronny and I had jumped up and hugged each other in the excitement.

That recollection, trudging up the staircase, was the first bout of nostalgia in my life. I would never catch up to Ronny as I wouldn't even get to high school for another year. And while Ronny had always wanted to go to law school, I still hadn't a clue about my future. That made adulthood seem farther away and more frightening. When Ronny had time he would tell me about weird court cases where mice were found in Coke bottles and men had sex with women they didn't know were dead. Once he had brought home a book on criminal evidence illustrated with photographs of shootings, stabbings, decapitations, but at the last moment he had changed his mind and wouldn't let me see it.

At the top of the stairs I turned past my parents' bedroom with its private bath, past the walk-in closets, the sewing room and the bathroom that Ronny and I shared with its separate sinks. The hall was bare, for the decorator, Dell, hadn't gotten here yet. That I hadn't told Ronny about Andrea Rapkin bothered me, although I must have had lots of minor secrets in the past that were already forgotten. But Andrea was different, she was the centre of my waking and increasingly my sleeping life. Andrea was

what I got up in the morning for, what I did my homework for, why I scrutinized my complexion in the mirror.
Ronny couldn't have been much help as he had never had
a girlfriend or even gone on a date. That was why my
mother watched him go off to those law-school parties. But
I also enjoyed having a secret from him, for it meant that I
had a separate life too, a life that nobody suspected. Andrea
Rapkin's eyes may have made me her slave, but they had
also made me free.

As Ronny's door was closed I had to juggle the milk
glass and the plate in one hand while I turned the knob. He
sat at his desk, the high intensity lamp burning a circle
around his face and elbows propped over an open volume.
Although his classes were over, he still had a big paper to
write. "Hi, Matt," he said.

"Hi, Ronny."

He took the cake and the milk from me and emptied
half the glass. Ronny's room looked like a temporary
refuge, with its boxes piled in the corner and the ham radio
balanced on top, dangling wires. I couldn't understand why
he had never fully unpacked, only that it made me uneasy.
He pushed a corner of the sponge cake into his mouth,
dropping crumbs. "Did you hear who's coming to speak at
school?" he mumbled.

"No." We didn't hear much about the law school over
at J. R. Henry.

"Kissinger, Henry Kissinger. The foreign-policy advisor.
Student Council's paying him a bundle. Some of the
students are organizing a petition to keep him out."

"He's an American." I said this to show that I was worthy of being spoken to.

"Only Nixon's right-hand man. Some students say he's a murderer, on account of Cambodia, and don't think he should be let into the country. They're passing out these stories from radical papers."

"What are you going to do?" I looked at Ronny wiping the remains of the demolished cake from his mouth. Before this year he had rarely read a newspaper and always said that politics was a bore. Instead, he used to read *Scientific American*.

"Maybe I'll write a letter to the Council. The point is to make a statement without infringing on freedom of speech." He gulped down the rest of the milk. "I said I had something for you, didn't I?"

"Yeah." I felt suddenly shy; I didn't want anything. Ronny reached into his knapsack on the floor and pulled out a paperback, its cover held together by Scotch tape.

"I bought this in a used bookshop on Queen Street. *All Quiet on the Western Front*. It's just about the greatest anti-war novel ever written. And it's about *Germans*."

Later I lay in bed, the flannel blanket pulled right up over my head. When I opened my eyes I could see the light from the aquarium filtered through the blanket. Ronny was still working — when I had gotten up to go to the bathroom the light showed under his door. What he had said about infringing on freedom of speech had sounded to me like the most profound idea ever conceived. Who had told him about this German book, I wondered, or had he found it on his own? I wasn't thinking about reading it (I wouldn't for years), I was judging whether *All Quiet on the Western Front* would make an impression on Andrea Rapkin, were she to see me reading it, say, in the cafeteria at lunch time while eating my peanut butter and banana sandwich. The only problem was that we had different lunch periods. In any case, I wasn't sure that I wanted to impress Andrea, not exactly. What I wanted was for her to know me as I was, for it seemed only logical that if I loved her then she ought to love me too, if she ever stopped to think about it. Otherwise too much of the energy in the universe would be wasted. Of course Andrea was of a different quality from me, but in science all kinds of laws existed about different substances being of equal value. There ought to be similar laws of love or else our hearts would float aimlessly about, the way our bodies would without gravity.

If I closed my eyes I could conjure up Andrea: tangled auburn hair, large eyes in a narrowing face to an almost pointed chin, dark eyebrows. She was a tiny girl, her arms like Bangladesh children in *Life* magazine, her shoulder blades as angular as the struts of a kite. On her third finger she wore a ring made from the handle of her baby spoon. I did not think of her body as unfinished or still changing to womanhood. She was just Andrea, as if she would remain always the way I first saw her. She was easy to imagine because for the last nine months she had sat directly in front of me in Mr Callaghan's grade-eight history class and I, after having fallen in love the first week of September, had taken care to memorize her every feature. But I didn't just know her physically, superficially (physical appearance was superficial, wasn't it?); I knew her inside as well, I knew her soul. I was sure I knew her soul. It pained me most deeply that my own remained closed to her.

Being able to imagine Andrea so clearly came in handy at night when I liked to think about her. These night daydreams, although mortifying, were irresistible. They usually started with a chance meeting by her locker when I would say,

"Andrea?"

And she would say,

"Uh-huh, Matthew?"

and look into my eyes. For the first time she would suspect my feelings and something would stir within her. The rest I had mapped out pretty thoroughly. The school dance, the first date (a chaste goodnight kiss), the passionate embrace, right through to marriage. Every night I ran the scenes over and over, replaying favourites like the ultimate, the wedding, and adding minor variations. It never seemed strange to me that two thirteen-year-olds should be standing under the *chupah*. Sometimes I wondered if I had already jinxed myself, if something could never happen once it had been turned into fantasy. But I couldn't stop. I even had a scene of our first love-making, beautiful and tender but darkly lit as, despite a knowledge of the clinical procedures of the act, I always suffered a failure of the imagination.

After Andrea and I had been married for the third time, I looked over to the small electric clock with the glow-dial on the night-table. It was after two in the morning. These dreams were becoming obsessive, lasting longer each night so that I would wake up in the morning, groggy from lack of sleep. I got up to go to the bathroom — Ronny's light was off now — and came back to bed.

∽

The bell rang, three long and penetrating clangs, and students slowed their cross-field chases or let handballs die against the wall as a movement began towards the open doors of the school. The sky over the field was a whitish blue and an airplane puttered across it like a toy. That morning the air carried such a scent of summer that it made even me want to bolt suddenly away, anywhere.

"Come on," said Howard Klapperman, sliding off the tree stump at the field's edge where we always sat and which we considered our own possession. "We'll be late for home room." But he immediately began chipping at the packed earth with his heel. "Look, ants!" Howard was ridiculously, uselessly tall and his bellbottom corduroys were an inch too short, making him look even longer. He had a hard time sitting still in class and had developed a neat trick of making his desk appear to levitate by raising his knees. His hair was straight and he was allowed to wear it longer than I was mine, over his ears and past his collar.

"You should see these ants run."

"Leave them alone," I said, slipping off the stump. "I thought you didn't want to be late for homeroom."

We hurried to join the last stragglers through the doors to the back stairwell where the cement-block walls had been painted by students to look like Peter Max posters.

"What day is it?" Howard asked as we were about to separate, he to his homeroom on the first floor, me to the second.

"Day four," I said.

"Shit, I've got French first thing. When's math?"

"Before first lunch."

"See you then."

J. R. Henry Junior High was considered an "advanced" school in the public system, the product of a liberalizing of educational values that had begun in the sixties and would reverse again a few years after us. We had an eight-day week so that we wouldn't always have the same line-up of subjects. Howard and I had gym together, and mathematics. We hated gym, but math class was based on the "open concept." Instead of regular rows we sat at round tables, working independently on math "notebooks," the teacher available only as a resource. Our teacher, Mr Aziz, sat with his feet propped on his desk reading *Sports Illustrated* or shooting paper basketballs off the blackboard and into the waste can. I sat at the same table as Howard, Jeff Engel, and Rudy Feinberg. We traded jokes, played table hockey with quarters, and argued whether Miss Owen, the librarian, could be called a genuine schizophrenic according to the *Webster's* definition. At the end of each month we would swap answers, making sure our notebooks didn't come out looking identical. The sharing made my marks lower than what I could have done on my own, but on the other hand we kept Rudy Feinberg from flunking. Some days when I felt particularly low on account of Andrea Rapkin and didn't feel like talking, Howard would divert the others from noticing. Howard was good about that; he considered it a privilege to know my secret.

On day four I didn't have history until last period. Mr Callaghan was, like most teachers it seemed, a strange man. His shining scalp was bordered on either side by a stiff crest of hair and he wore a bristly little moustache over his mouth that hardly moved as he talked, like the mouths of the characters in the Saturday morning cartoon *Clutch Cargo*. He was a holdout from the old teaching methods and appeared every day in a tweed jacket with suede elbows over an orange turtleneck. At the moment he had his back to the class to draw on the board in his deliberate hand one of his Course of History charts. This one was labelled "The Road to War" and consisted of a line marked 1933 at one end and 1939 at the other, with little slashes in between. Mr Callaghan began to write along the slashes "Burning of the Reichstag" and "Munich Agreement." The other students were busy copying down — Stephen Weiss in the next row over used a ruler and three coloured pens.

I tapped the shoulder in front of me, a shoulder covered in a yellow blouse with red and white dots.

"What, Matthew?"

Andrea Rapkin half turned in her seat to look at me. She smelled fresh, like lemons. Her gaze went over my shoulder and then back to me, hardly hiding her impatience. When she tapped the end of her pencil against her lower lip a pain contracted my heart and spread like a stain. I wanted to say her name aloud, over and over.

"What do you want, Matthew?"

"Eraser," I said. "Do you have an eraser?"

"Hold on."

She fished in her pencil case. "Here, but I want it back," she said, holding it over my open palm.

"Guaranteed . . . Andrea."

She dropped it and turned around again to copy down the chart. The eraser was shaped like a poodle with googly eyes pasted on. "What a great eraser, Andrea —"

Mr Callaghan turned around. Scowling, he wiped his nose, leaving a whitish smudge of chalk.

"Is somebody talking?"

Andrea whispered. "Shit."

I cleared my throat. "Me, sir. I was just borrowing something."

"Well, keep quiet about it."

"Sir?"

"What is it, Matthew?"

Mr Callaghan waited. What I said arose from no natural bravado, breaking as it did my code of anonymity, but was a gift for Andrea, a token of love.

"Mr Callaghan, you have chalk on your nose."

The class roared.

After the final bell of the day, Howard and I met, as usual, in the field behind the school. We stood with our knapsacks piled on the tree stump and watched two football teams scrapple for ground between the goal posts. Mr Delmonico, the gym teacher, blew his whistle and made sharp arm movements like a professional referee. But the teams in their grass-stained uniforms and bruised helmets looked small and clumsy, and the ball kept squirting out of the hands of whichever team was supposed to possess it, dissolving the formations into a desultory free-for-all. Nobody watched from the other side of the field except for a couple of grade sevens whom Mr Delmonico had coerced into holding the down markers.

Howard shoved the blade of his Swiss army knife into the bark of the stump and twisted it. "She just gave you her eraser?" he said.

"Not gave exactly. I sort of forgot to give it back."

"What are you going to do with it?"

"I don't know, just keep it for a while. Don't think I'm stupid, Howard, I know that it's just an inanimate object. But she bought it and used it and leant it to me. That makes it almost mysterious, I guess. Anyway, what else do I have except my suffering? God, she's so beautiful — inside I mean."

Howard bunged his knife into the bark. "Jesus, Matthew, you really are obsessed."

"You think so?"

"Are you kidding? How long have you been in love with Andrea?"

"Nine months and three weeks. That is, nine months and three weeks of hell."

I felt a twinge of shame for the dramatics, but Howard ate it up. "Wow," he said. "That must be some kind of school record. You ought to have your name engraved on a plaque and hung in the cafeteria, right next to Bruce Mackenzie's long-jump record."

"I wouldn't want a plaque," I mused, as if seriously considering the proposition. "This is a private burden."

Howard nodded. He didn't think to ask why, if it was

so private, I told him everything. Having Howard was a pleasant part of the enterprise, as if through him I could admire my own condition. But when it came to really expressing how I felt, words just failed. The version that Howard received sounded to my own ears pathetically melodramatic.

Howard didn't notice any of that. Instead, he did something I always enjoyed: he tested my devotion.

"Matt, now that summer's coming on and school's going to be out next week, aren't you getting tired of thinking about Andrea all the time?"

"No."

"You mean you don't feel like doing something else for a change? Like joining a basketball team or going to camp like I am or anything?"

"That's just it — I can't do anything else. This isn't a choice, Howard, we've gone over this. All that I can do is love Andrea."

"Wow," he said again.

"I have to get home. Let's take the shortcut." Without waiting for an answer I started down the hill to the first set of fenced-in backyards. We'd long ago discovered a route to my street, sneaking through gaps in fences and sliding beneath side windows. As I was about to jump the first fence, Howard said to me:

"Matthew, have you ever masturbated?"

"Get out of here."

"I mean it. Ernie Shore told me he does it every night."

"He didn't."

"Swear to God. Told me his dad has a stack of *Playboy*

magazines in the basement closet behind his tuxedo. Ernie does it right in the closet. Last winter his mother opened the door, looking for her mink stole."

We crept along a narrow path between two houses with identical round turrets over their garages. The house on the right kept a harmless but yappy cocker spaniel that was better left undisturbed. After we had passed, Howard continued defensively, "Lots of guys do it. It feels good. The first time my brother did it he looked at his sperm under my dad's microscope." (Howard's father was an ear, nose, and throat specialist.) "He could see them swimming around."

"He smeared it on a slide? Yech."

"That's the scientific method."

"I really don't want to talk about this."

"You mean you really never did it? Maybe when you were thinking of Andrea —"

"Watch what you're saying."

"Okay, don't get mad. Listen, you want to come over tonight and watch *Laugh-In*? Come on, Matthew —"

But I was already running across my own backyard.

Ronny didn't come home for dinner; he telephoned to say he would be staying late at the law school. My mother and father and I ate in the kitchen, and to fill in the absence I found myself talking about anything that came into my head. For dessert my mother served strawberries in glasses, mine with sugar sprinkled over them. I was about to excuse myself and head up to finish my homework when my father rose from the table and awkwardly cleared his throat.

"Matthew, I want you to come into the living room."

"Okay, Dad." As he seemed to be waiting for me I slid from behind the table and went out the kitchen door, my father and mother following like we were in a parade. Had I done anything wrong? My parents did not mete out formal punishments. In the living room the television had been left on and Walter Cronkite, my father's favourite, was reading the news. Perhaps they had found out about Andrea Rapkin and disapproved. If that was the case I would remain steadfast. The situation might even be reminiscent of *Romeo and Juliet*, about which I had to write an assignment for tomorrow's English class. Of course I realized it wasn't really the same; the Capulets and the Montagues were rival families, whereas Andrea's father and my mother sat on the same local committee of the United Jewish Appeal.

My father halted behind me to look at the television, as if he had forgotten why we were here. Then he gazed at me the way he usually did before giving me a kiss, fished into his pocket, and pulled out a flash of gold.

"This is for you, Matthew."

He held towards me a pocket watch. Chainless, a convex circle fitting easily into his hand. I took it from him — the watch was surprisingly light and thin — and examined the case, ribbed with parallel lines that my fingertips could just distinguish. "Push that sort of button at the top," my father said, and when I did the front tipped open to reveal a face the colour of ivory, marked by roman numerals. The hands looked like elongated diamonds with the centres cut out, tiny wrought iron. I noticed that the watch was ticking; I had been hearing it all the time.

"It was my father's watch, your Zeyde's. He bought it in Switzerland on a selling trip before the war. Here, press the button a little harder."

I did and the back of the watch jumped open. There wasn't much to see except the steel back protecting the insides and an engraving of two small medallions. Beside the medallions was engraved LEFEVRES ET FRERES and beneath that, GENEVE 1928.

"Do you remember your Zeyde?"

"Yes, I remember him," I answered, annoyed at the question.

"I didn't know whether to give it to you or Ronny, but somehow I thought you would appreciate it, and Ronny agreed."

"Do you like it, Matt?" asked my mother.

"Yes." I was closing the front and back and popping them open again. When I looked up at my father he had tears in his eyes. I prepared for him to hug me. "Thank you," I mumbled into his shoulder.

Almost immediately after, I went up to my room, closed the door, and began to work, the watch with its face open propped against the *Webster's Dictionary* on the desk. My father had said that he had meant to give me the watch on the day of my Bar Mitzvah but he didn't explain why he hadn't. On that day last August the new house had filled with hundreds of guests. I had invited few friends, having already drifted away from the old neighbourhood but as yet knowing no one in the new. For presents I received money, a chess set, a copy of Herman Wouk's *This Is My God*, and three pairs of binoculars. Standing at the door and greeting the guests, I had hated my parents for making me go through with this and, as soon as I could, slipped away to my room and lay on my bed reading old issues of *Mad* magazine. I only came down again when the guests were gone and the family — mother and father, Ronny, Uncle Norman, Aunt Ida and Mosey, and my grandmother — sat in the dishevelled living room, the men with their ties askew, the women with their shoes kicked off, and my grandmother asleep. It was only then, as my parents looked up at me, that I realized the ordeal had been worse for them than for me, that they had been strangers in their own house.

The assignment seemed to take forever to compose, perhaps because I kept glancing at the time on the face of the watch and listening to its ticking, a remarkable sound, comfortable as a heart beat. My father had never mentioned its existence before and it occurred to me that the watch might be the only heirloom the family possessed, as my grandmother had lost her original wedding band years ago. This then was the only object that had travelled even as far as three generations. I put down my pen and picked up the watch, pressed the button beneath the triangle meant for the chain, and read again the engraved words on the back: GENEVE 1928. I knew almost nothing of my family's story other than that we were Jews like other Jews. What my family's life had been like before my grandfather brought them to Canada I had little idea, for nobody ever spoke of it. Instead, they talked about the retail sales market, a new restaurant opening, a movie. An ongoing joke was to kid Aunt Ida for spending so much time at the Y. My father, I calculated, must have been about my age when he left for Canada. It was as if I were to move to another country tomorrow and never again think of the life I'd lived until then.

But here was this watch, ticking steadily in my hand. When I turned the knob I could hear the spring — if that's what it was — winding. Perhaps the watch hadn't been in my father's possession all these years but had materialized out of the past, carrying a secret message inside: GENEVE 1928.

After finishing the assignment I went downstairs again and watched television with my parents, one of those detective shows my mother liked in which policemen were always chasing pimps in white suits down alleys. My father, reading glasses balanced on his nose, flipped through the shoe manufacturers' catalogues, working on next spring's orders. Ronny phoned again to say he would be even later, having gone to a classmate's house to study. I kissed my mother and father and went back upstairs.

In bed, in the dark, I watched the aquarium against the wall. The light was out but whenever the heater went on, a little red bulb made visible the silhouettes of the zebra fish and swordtails. At various times I had also owned angels, kissing gouramis, neon tetras, puffers, silver dollars, catfish, loaches, newts, but they had all died. Watching, I tried to remember my grandfather, who I knew had once made hats and smoked cigarettes. I could call up only one clear memory of him, but even that memory was suspicious for I saw myself too, as if in a film. In the background was Crystal Beach, umbrellas and changing huts in the distance, and Zeyde standing in his bathing trunks and a cotton hat, his hands on his hips. The hair on his chest was gray and curly. I appeared, running diagonally across the frame, my feet sinking in the sand, when Zeyde grabbed me and lifted me in the air. I was about four years old, with a blossom of dark hair, pudgy cheeks. I struggled out of his arms, ran out of the frame, leaving him alone on the beach.

The final image made me, lying in bed, feel guilty and sad. A swift, childish rejection of my grandfather, a desertion. The only memory I had of him was of running away.

Turning onto my stomach I felt the coolness of the pillow compress beneath my face. I didn't want to think about my grandfather anymore, but about Andrea, and I wondered how the watch could help me win her. Perhaps if I just showed it to her she wouldn't realize its value. But what was its value and how could I convey that to her? Perhaps it was like a bottle from which could be drawn a genie, if only one knew how.

My usual nightly imaginings of Andrea began: from the first high-school dance to the afternoon after school by the tree stump where I proposed to her. During the second run I slowed the story down to watch Andrea unbutton her polka-dot blouse and slide it from her narrow shoulders. This afternoon I had lied to Howard Klapperman; I had discovered masturbation one night while Andrea was unfastening her thin, white bra and I, pushing heatedly against the bed, had found a surprised sound in my throat. Afterwards, with the bathroom door locked, I had washed out my pyjamas in the sink and wondered if I had desecrated my love for Andrea.

I had done it several times since. It seemed that while I couldn't imagine the actual act of making love, my body didn't require my imagination to go that far. I knew what the dream-Andrea looked like under that blouse, and how her eyes would slowly close and open again.

Only I didn't want a substitute, a dream-Andrea, no matter how yielding. I wanted the real Andrea, even if she refused to follow the story. I kicked the covers off the bed and looked at the face of the watch, propped against the glow-dial of the electric clock. Somehow the watch would help me to show her just how much love a boy could feel.

∽

The two men in goggles, hip-waders, and rubber gloves cleaned the swimming pool of its winter sludge, one using a large broom to sweep down the walls and the other aiming the spray from the nozzle of a hose. Home from an uneventful day at school, I watched from the glass doors of the living room as each sweep of the broom left a highway of shining tile, like the road to Oz. Other pools in the neighbourhood had been cleaned weeks ago but my father had just gotten around to phoning the pool company.

My father would be home at six o'clock. Because my mother wouldn't allow him to stay late, he had to go in early and rose every morning before the rest of the house. That was why he fell asleep in his chair, watching the late news on the CBC.

My father was not cut out for retail. Once, during a visit to his office near the lakeshore, I saw a man come in without knocking and begin shouting at my father, something about a cancelled order of ladies' slippers. My father couldn't deal with such a brute, he just listened and, when the man had spent his energy, made him a cup of tea. Fortified, the man started shouting again and I wished I hadn't come, not for my sake but my father's.

He had been made to take over the business by his own father. My grandfather couldn't tolerate working with Uncle Norman and told him so; and as for Aunt Ida, in spite of her head for business, she was a woman and ought not to deal with such responsibility. Anything more about it I didn't know, and that much only because of some chance remark at the dinner table. Learning anything about the family was like finding stray pieces of a jigsaw puzzle, the design of which I couldn't imagine. My grandfather must have been very different from my father; perhaps he had been one of the shouters. Would I have liked him? Would I have been afraid of him?

My mother said dinner wouldn't be for another hour and so I walked to the corner and took the bus to Shoprite Plaza. A short strip of stores anchored by a Kmart, it had recently been eclipsed by a new indoor mall with cinemas and both Eaton's and Simpsons. The plaza was deserted and shabby: garbage bins brimming, one shop empty and with a crack in the glass covered in tape, like stitches. I walked to Reisman's Jewellery and looked in the window where some wedding rings rotated on a stand and a row of Timex watches had their prices marked down.

Mr Reisman sat at the back, peering through a small eyeglass, and when he looked up at my approach the glass stayed in his eye. He didn't recognize me from the time I had accompanied my father on an errand to get a brooch repaired. Taking the eyeglass out, he brushed his white hair from his forehead.

"Yes?"

"I want to buy a chain." I pulled the watch from my pocket and deposited it on the counter. Mr Reisman screwed up his eye as if the glass were still in it and picked up the watch. He scrutinized its front and back, listened to the ticking, shook it, read the engraving.

"Are you sure this is your watch?" he said, keeping it in his hand.

"Yes, it's mine."

"You want to sell it?"

I was too surprised to answer and he read my silence as interest. "I could give you eight hundred dollars for it."

"I don't want to sell it. I just want a chain."

"All right. Just a minute." He took a key from somewhere and unlocked the back of the counter, from which he withdrew a velvet tray. "This one," he said, pointing to the first chain, "is gold plated. Ten dollars. This one is ten karat. Twenty-three dollars. And this one, which a watch like yours deserves, is twenty-four karat. Forty-five dollars."

I looked at the three chains. The twenty-four karat certainly looked the best, its colour almost as rich as the watch and brighter for its newness. But I had only twelve dollars in my wallet, money I'd been saving since Hanukah to buy a mask and fins for the pool.

"I'll take the ten-dollar chain," I said.

Mr Reisman shrugged, removed the chain from the velvet, and placed the tray back under the counter. I left the shop with the chain clipped to the watch at one end and a belt loop on my jeans at the other, the watch nestled in my pocket. Pausing before the empty storefront, I could just make out the reflection of the chain running from the loop to the top of the pocket. I pulled out the watch, snapped open the face, noted with satisfaction that I was late for dinner, and slipped it back again.

The family waited for me — not just my parents but my grandmother, Aunt Ida and Mosey, and Uncle Norman wearing a paisley shirt with wide lapels, picked out by his sister. The dinner settings had been switched from the kitchen to the dining room and I could tell by the way she bustled about that my mother wasn't pleased at the unexpected guests. Mosey was already at the table, a napkin tucked into his collar. And Aunt Ida, wearing a T-shirt emblazened with a marijuana leaf (she may not have known what it was) followed my mother about, recounting some incident from the bridal shop. "Can you believe some of these girls?" she said. "The world is changing and all they care about is Wedgwood."

"It's the way they were brought up," my mother said, softening. Her sister-in-law might get on her nerves but my mother knew it wasn't easy working in that shop and catering to women twenty-five years younger.

"If I was their age I wouldn't get married," Aunt Ida said. "The kids with their free love, they've got it right."

"Better not tell them at the Y," Uncle Norman winked at me, "or you'll have all the *alter kockers* chasing you around the track."

Uncle Norman and my father had the evening paper spread over the kitchen table. "Dad," I half-whispered, standing beside my father, "can I show them my watch?"

"What's that?"

"My watch."

As I pulled it part way out of my pocket my father stared without recognition. "Oh, sure," he said finally, turning back to the newspaper. "Go ahead."

But I didn't know what to do. I had been hoping my father would say something like, look, the family heirloom has been passed on, it's Matthew's now. Left to do it on my own, I felt suddenly shy.

"Look, Aunt Ida."

My voice came out as a squeak. "Yes, sweetheart," she said, turning from my mother, who was peering into a casserole on the stove.

"See what I've got." Eager now, I pulled up the chain. "It's Zeyde's old watch."

Aunt Ida screamed. Her hands went up to her face and she started to slump when my mother caught her around the waist. My father and Uncle Norman had to take Aunt Ida, now weeping like a crazy woman, into the living room. I stepped back against the refrigerator, still dangling the watch, to let them pass. When I followed, the watch back in my pocket, I could see Mosey at the dining-room table with the napkin arranged in his collar.

Dinner was delayed. Aunt Ida had to be laid on the sofa for almost an hour, a compress on her forehead and my mother stroking her hand. When things had quietened down, the others each took a look at the watch. "Sure, I used to wind it for him," Uncle Norman said and went to bring Mosey to his wife. My grandmother took it in her fleshy hands to feel its lightness. Ignoring her daughter's condition she made a shrill little laugh. "Ach, how that man enjoyed spoiling himself."

This was not, I felt, how a family ought to treat its only surviving remembrance. I had expected a certain quiet intensity, as if we could all see down a tunnel to a small and shining light. And I suppose I thought they might look at me differently too, more as an adult and also with sudden affection. Aunt Ida recovered enough to sit up and then come to the table with bloodshot eyes and skin pale as flour; for the first time she looked her forty-seven years. My father laid his palm on my shoulder on the way to his place at the table, a sign that what had occurred wasn't my fault. But that wasn't what I wanted from him; I knew even less now what this watch was good for.

"Soup?" Aunt Ida said as my mother served the first course. "Who thinks of eating soup in June?"

"It's cold," my mother said, her sympathy for Aunt Ida seeping away. "If you don't want it you can leave it."

Aunt Ida sipped the soup, slow as an invalid. But over the course of the meal her appetite returned and she joined the conversation, which had turned from real estate to music. She said, "Never has there been a singer as great as Streisand. Never."

"I still enjoy listening to Judy Garland," said my mother. "She was like a songbird."

"But not like Streisand."

"For my money," Uncle Norman said, "you cannot fully appreciate Streisand unless you are Jewish. It's as simple as that."

"And the Beatles," said Aunt Ida. "The Beatles and Streisand. They're the tops."

"And what about Burt Bacharach?" said my father.

"He's not a singer," said Aunt Ida. "He's a different category."

"When you're talented," my father said, "categories don't matter."

After dinner my mother served tea and ginger cookies in the living room and the evening was warm enough to open the sliding doors to the back garden. The television was on and as the sky outside darkened the screen grew brighter, its colours kaleidoscopic as Mosey changed the channel with the remote control. My homework wasn't finished because of the visit to the mall but I felt some obligation to my aunt and sat on the piano bench where I flipped idly through Ronny's long-unplayed music. Several cups of tea brought the colour back to Aunt Ida's cheeks while Uncle Norman was saying how he heard on the radio that *Life* magazine was in trouble and might stop publishing. The news saddened me, for not long ago the magazine had published a photograph of a turtle with two heads, full page.

"Dad" — to this day I do not understand my own nerve or stupidity — "when did Zeyde buy that watch?"

I watched my aunt in case she fell down again or started to scream, but she was listening to the television. "In Zurich," my father said, "on a selling trip. Actually, there's an interesting story about that watch." My ears pricked up. At last a story about our past, a fragment of history. "We left Brussels just before the Nazis. We had to leave all our possessions behind and my father asked our neighbour in the house attached to ours to look after things. Well, a few months later — we were staying near the Spanish border — your Zeyde decided that he wanted to check up on our property. I don't know how he did it, but he smuggled himself back into Belgium, went to our street, and discovered that the neighbour had stolen everything. They had a big argument and the neighbour said that if Zeyde didn't leave he'd sic the Nazis on him. So he left. The only thing he managed to take was that watch. Slipped it into his pocket when the neighbour wasn't looking. Then he came back to us. And as we never returned we lost everything we owned."

I sat listening, wordless. This was what I had hoped for: a story grand enough to fill the empty space of the past. My fingers slipped down my leg to feel the watch's outline in my pocket; I imagined that I could feel it ticking, like a pulse. Here was a witness of all that was lost . . .

"What nonsense."

It was Aunt Ida. Apparently she had been only half listening to the television.

"Matthew," my mother said, "would you close the sliding doors? It's starting to get chilly."

I went over to the doors but instead of closing them put my back to the screen. My father sat on the sofa, frowning. "What do you mean?" he said.

"I mean it's nonsense. Rubbish."

"Really, Ida!"

"You can't remember, you were too young. Do you really think that Pa would have been foolish enough to risk being shot by Nazis just to look at our property? He wasn't a stupid man, you must have seen that in some television show. I remember. Matthew, your Zeyde bought that watch from a Dutch refugee while we lived in the internment camp. The man needed money and he sold it to father for a low price, a bargain. That's the real story."

My father shook his head in astonishment. "I can't believe what I'm hearing. Ida, you've always had a vivid imagination but this takes the cake. You mean that our father would take advantage of a man in trouble and practically cheat him out of his watch? He wasn't that kind of person."

"Well, he wasn't an idiot, I can assure you of that. Norman, tell him the truth."

"Me? I don't remember anything. Mosey, turn up the television."

A tapping from behind made me turn around. A June bug was battering itself against the screen door. Then another drove into the screen and another.

"Ma?" Aunt Ida appealed.

My grandmother squinted fiercely. "This eye is bothering me again."

Upstairs, I fooled with my homework, sprawled across the bed with my shoes kicked off and my French notebook open. I filled in three wrong answers in a row, on purpose. Today was Tuesday, exactly one week before the final day of school. Next year I would have to work harder to get into the enriched courses at high school the year after, but that seemed so far away it was no more real than the past. To forget about everything, I started to think about

Andrea Rapkin, how when she knew the answer to one of Mr Callaghan's questions she would stretch her hand in the air and quiver in anticipation. Howard had told me that she had a younger brother who was "slow" and that on Saturday afternoons she took him to the movies. This showed her compassion and I wondered if she would like company. One day last week she had worn sandals to school and I had seen her narrow feet with high arches and the little toes turned in. They were beautiful feet.

"Doing your homework like a good boy?" Over my shoulder I saw Aunt Ida standing in the doorway. "I just wanted to say good night." As she came in I hoped that she wouldn't apologize or say how wrong my father was, and when she sat on the bed and ruffled my hair I knew that she would do neither. "You're my favourite, you know that?" she said. "Like my own little boy. Only you're not little anymore, you're going to be fourteen. What are you studying?"

"French."

"Do you like languages?"

Her face looked haggard, bruised. I knew then that a man like Mosey could never have satisfied a woman like Ida. Whatever the truth, history had left her with so little. She stroked the hair from my forehead, and looking down I had the nauseous desire to bury my face between her breasts.

"Sweetheart," she said, shifting away, "one day you're going to make some lucky girl very happy."

On Friday, the expectation of summer vacation beginning the next week was like the funnel of a twister hovering over the school; in a moment the pressure might blow off the roof. Only in history class, which I had after home, room, could Mr Callaghan bring order to the students merely by standing before us and dabbing at his moustache with a handkerchief. When the class had settled down, he refolded the handkerchief, placed his hands behind his back, and smiled.

"Next Tuesday I have a little treat for the last day of school. A test."

The class groaned. "None of that, now." Silence again. "This test will count and I expect all of you to be prepared. So let's get on with the lesson. Who can tell me about Prime Minister Mackenzie King and the Canadian war effort?"

Andrea Rapkin's hand rose. Hunched over my notebook, I traced a line around the poodle eraser with the googly eyes. I wasn't in the mood to think about Mackenzie King, and besides, Howard had told me that the prime minister had been an anti-Semite, although Howard couldn't be quoted as a reliable historical source. Andrea was talking, her head tilted to one side so that I could see her small and perfect ear, naked of earring but marked by an impressed point where the lobe had been pierced. She wore her hair in a braid today and I could see light down on her neck. It looked soft.

Mr Callaghan asked another question but I didn't care, not with Andrea sitting in front of me, and I having no right to whisper into her ear the sort of words that only lovers understand. Instead, I let my mind drift and thought of Ronny, who had come into my room last night. At the dinner table — for the first time in weeks he had eaten with us — Ronny had talked about Quebec and how it was only right that a people with a separate culture should hunger for political autonomy. My father, who disliked disruption of any kind, disagreed, but he listened to what Ronny had to say and I could see he was impressed with how exactly Ronny expressed himself. Meanwhile, my mother, who believed that politics meant voting the same way as her husband, used the opportunity to soak up Ronny's presence before he disappeared again.

Later, when Ronny came into my room, I was supposed to be doing my homework. Instead, I was dancing in front of the closet mirror while my mother's portable radio-recorder on the dresser was tuned to the CHUM Top 40 countdown. Andrea Rapkin was throwing a party the day after the end of school and I wanted to be ready in case of an invitation. That was likely only if one of her real friends couldn't make it, but an increasingly desperate belief in destiny drove me to the agony of watching my feet shuffle and my hands saw the air. I simply couldn't dance. Perhaps with the lights down low and the music up and Andrea dancing with me —

I managed to stop and pretend to look for something in the closet before Ronny came through the door. "What's that junk?" he said, turning off the radio. "You shouldn't listen to trash, Matt."

"I don't. I mean, sometimes I do just to know the names of the songs."

"It isn't necessary to conform to the other kids."

I resented that, for I *did* want to do what the other kids did, at least some of the time. Only lately had Ronny, on the rare occasions we talked, begun to offer these sermons for my benefit. "I have to finish my homework," I said.

"Okay." And in a single motion he left the room, closing the door behind him. I stood looking at the door and wishing he would come back. It was the first time I had ever turned him away; before, I would have dropped everything to spend a few minutes with Ronny. Perhaps I was angry: at dinner Ronny had announced his acquisition of a summer research position with one of his professors, which for me meant only that we would not spend those months playing our pool games like last year. And now when would we talk next, in days or weeks? Although I could not have said it, I felt as if I were looking into the beginning of a gulf that would widen as we grew older.

"Copy this down, it might be on the test," Mr Callaghan said and began to draw a line on the chalkboard. Another Course of History chart, this one entitled "Canada at War." While Andrea was busy scribbling, I took the watch from my pocket, unclipped the chain, and laid it, closed, on my desk. I traced its shape in my notebook next to the poodle eraser. Andrea turned and as I placed my hands under my desk, as if I had been guilty of something, she looked down at the watch, attracted by its ticking. Then she looked up at me, raising her eyes slowly. My heart pounded. She gazed at me for what seemed a full minute and then reached over, picked up the poodle eraser, and turned back again.

The last period of the day, gym, gave me the unexpected opportunity of seeing Andrea again, for the folding partition that separated the boys' and girls' sides of the gymnasium had been mechanically withdrawn. The boys who lined the wall of their side wore J.R. Henry T-shirts, blue shorts, white socks, and sneakers. The girls, against their own wall, had on one-piece gym suits with puffed sleeves and elastic waists, leaving their arms and legs bare. Between us was strewn an array of gymnastics equipment — vaulting horses, bars, and mats.

"I hate gymnastics," said Howard, slouched next to the wall beside me. I was scratching my leg self-consciously and taking furtive glances at Andrea. "Why can't we just play rugby? Look at Sheryl Mann by the water fountain. She's got the biggest knockers in grade eight. Hey, Matthew, you want to sleep over at my place Saturday night?"

"Listen up, people." It was Mr Delmonico, the boys' gym teacher, striding alongside Miss Cartwright to the middle of the gym. Mr Delmonico's hairy legs made the girls titter. He favoured the athletic boys but left the rest of us alone so long as we didn't just stand around. The gymnastics program was part of a new national fitness scheme, the end of which was a short routine that each of us would present to the class. I hadn't thought about mine much, but I wasn't scheduled until Monday and figured on an allergy attack to keep me safe in bed that afternoon.

"All right," Mr Delmonico bellowed. "I don't want a lot of time-wasting. We've got a dozen presentations to get through, so listen up. The order today will be —"

And he ran off a list of names. Including mine. The noise of the gym faded away, the blood emptied from my legs, the lights dimmed. Then it all came roaring back. Howard was yanking my arm and urging me to tell Mr Delmonico that a mistake had been made, but I couldn't move. The first student was already walking up to the parallel bars. She began with four neat moves, leading into a series of somersaults. Some of the other girls applauded. The other routines I saw in a daze while Howard tried to get me ready by talking me through my own. At the sound of my name my legs wavered and then took me to the centre of the gymnasium floor. Mr Delmonico stood beneath a basketball hoop, clipboard in hand. I didn't want to, but I couldn't help looking at Andrea. She leaned against the wall with one foot tucked up, her arms crossed over her chest, and her hair tied back from her face. She looked small next to the other girls. She moved her fingers; it might have been meant as a wave, but I wasn't sure.

I stretched out my arms, took a deep breath, and was off: a jump over the horse, a jerky series of rolls on the mats, a walk down the balance beam from which I teetered, raising giggles from the girls. One by one I performed the minimum requirements of the routine without energy or grace or nerve. In my final move I realized with horror that my program was too short — I'd been up for only a couple of minutes. Turning, I saw the trampoline, made an immediate decision to use it, and was already sprinting forward before considering my ignorance of the proper mount. So I simply leapt, straight ahead, landing on all fours and hooking one foot in the springs. I got up and began to bounce, slowly at first but going higher and higher, the eyes from both sides of the gym following me up and down. It was at the apex of my bouncing that I realized I did not know any trampoline moves, not a flip or a tumble. I slowed down, the height of my bounce shrinking until I stood, grinning uncontrollably, my arms extended and the trampoline sagging beneath my feet. From what seemed a mile away came the sound of Howard's applause.

∽

The last weekend of the school year brought the first truly hot weather of the summer and by ten o'clock Saturday morning we were sitting on the patio drinking glasses of iced tea that my mother carried to us on a tray. The portable radio-recorder on the porch wall played a Diane Warwick song. For once my grandmother didn't feel the necessity of wearing a sweater over her shoulders, and with her rhinestone-studded sunglasses she looked like a cross between an aging Hollywood star and Buddha. At the patio table my father and Uncle Norman and Mosey shared the weekend newspaper, the three of them in Bermuda shorts and rubber sandals.

"D-do you see this?" said Mosey "Here, in the b-business section. F-franchise — it's the wave of the f-future."

A news report began on the radio. The deep-voiced announcer spoke of a Viet Cong ambush in some delta that left three helicopters burning and eighteen American soldiers dead. There was speculation of an American pull-out. Aunt Ida got up to turn the dial to a Benny Goodman swing tune. "I don't want to hear anymore," she said.

"Those poor boys, it's so horrible. Just last night they showed a boy who'd lost both his legs and I started to cry, didn't I, Mosey? Why don't they stop, it's just awful and I can't take it any more."

"Ida, you're going to make yourself sick," said my father. "Come, sit under the umbrella." My mother took Ida by the arm and led her to a chair. "You don't want to get too much sun yet, or you'll burn." Aunt Ida wore cut-off shorts and a bikini top and her hair must have been tinted this week as it looked redder than usual. She smiled at my mother and allowed a pillow to be placed behind her head.

"Matthew," Uncle Norman said, "when you were little I could wiggle one finger and you would start to laugh, that's how ticklish you were."

He held up a finger and started to wiggle it.

"That's right," Aunt Ida said. "And you sat on my lap and let me hug you all I wanted. But now you're all frowns and secrets —"

"How about some more iced tea, Ida?" my mother said.

"No, we ought to be going for lunch soon. Ma, where do you want to go?"

"What?" My grandmother looked up, gripping the arms of the lawn chair as if someone were going to drag her away.

"Where do you want to go for lunch?"

"Don't ask me. I made enough decisions in this life."

"Norman?"

"I'm easy." He was standing behind my father, reading a headline over his shoulder.

"Then stay here," my mother said. "I'll throw something together."

"We wouldn't think of it," said Aunt Ida. "It's too much trouble. Mosey, you choose."

My grandmother chortled. "You ask a man who can't even make a living?"

Mosey looked at us and raised his open palms as if he were pleading or attempting levitation. "Why . . . why . . ."

"Please." My mother hardly concealed her impatience. "It's no trouble. I'll make some tuna and egg salad and we have fresh bagels."

"Poppyseed?" Uncle Norman asked.

"Well, I insist on helping," Aunt Ida said without rising. "Such a nice day. Who really wants to sit in a stuffy restaurant?"

We ate lunch on the patio, all except Ronny, who woke up late and went off to the library, and afterwards Uncle Norman and Mosey went inside to watch a football game on television. Aunt Ida and my father dragged another cot down to the pool and turned towards the sun. They had forgotten about their disagreement over the watch; my father rubbed suntan oil onto her back. As I looked down at them from the patio, the sun appeared from behind a cloud, glinting off the pool's surface, blinding. In the starburst behind my closing eyelids my grandfather appeared, his feet in the sand, catching me in his arms and then losing me. I played it backwards and forwards: catching me, losing me, catching me, losing me.

On the porch my mother fussed over a row of flower

pots, breaking up the earth with a trowel. She seemed happy on her own and only glanced now and again at my dozing grandmother. Over twenty years ago my grandmother and grandfather and even my Aunt Ida had tried to stop my parents' marriage. I knew this from a chat with my mother one winter afternoon while she cooked in the kitchen and seemed to forget that I, home from school with a cold, was her listener. My mother came from Montreal, had no money or education, was the daughter of greeners. Poor as my father's own family was, they thought she wasn't good enough. My grandfather was the worst, the most stubborn and insulting. But my father married her anyway in perhaps the first and last disobedient act of his life. As for my mother, she served, she comforted, she made a second home for my father's family. But it was she, I am sure, who took that wedding portrait from the mantle and put it back in the J&B Whisky box in the basement.

Did she learn to love my grandfather, I wondered. Did he, before the final day of his life, of which I had no recollection, say to her: forgive me. I didn't know and I couldn't ask. My mother suddenly looked up from the mixing bowl (she was making a chiffon cake) and stopped talking. How strange this silence seemed when I recalled that insistent Hebrew school lesson — that the Jews never forgot their history, that next to the word of God it was their greatest passion and possession. Weren't tears and forgiveness or not forgiving part of history? If memory and faith made us Jews, then what were we who neglected to pray and who refused to remember?

They stayed all afternoon and into the evening. I went upstairs and spent an hour on a two-page essay on the Canadian war industry so that if I received a good mark I could casually drop my paper in front of Andrea Rapkin's desk. By now I had dropped all reservations about such tricks. When I came downstairs again the family was in the living room watching Walt Disney. Aunt Ida flipped through my father's shoe catalogues. "Norman," she said, "are you getting hungry?"

"A little."

"Where do you want to go for supper?"

"I'm easy."

"Mosey?"

"Where — wherever . . ."

"How about the deli at the mall?"

"Too greasy," Uncle Norman said.

"Chinese food?"

"Feh," from my grandmother.

My father gave my mother a pleading look. She turned away for a moment and then, calm again, turned back. "I broiled an extra chicken yesterday. I can make some vegetables with it."

"Don't be crazy," Ida said. "We absolutely refuse to impose on you again."

Half an hour later we sat down to dinner, cramped around the kitchen table. Aunt Ida, pulling apart a wing with her long-nailed fingers, said to my father, "So, do you remember now about Pa buying the watch from that Dutchman?"

Surprised, I looked up from my plate. My father said, "No, you're still wrong, Ida. In fact, there are a lot of things I remember. I might even write my memoirs."

"Your memoirs!" Aunt Ida howled. "Is your life as interesting as Frank Sinatra's?"

"I remember our neighbour in Brussels," Uncle Norman said. As always he sat beside his mother so he could cut her food. "A man with a wart on his chin. But he wasn't a Gentile, he was a Jew. So. if he did steal our property after we left, then it was a Jew stealing from another Jew."

My father squinted up at the skylight and cleared his throat. He looked embarrassed or perhaps angry, I couldn't tell.

⌀

Whenever I slept over at Howard Klapperman's house we didn't use his room, which had only a single bed, but the guest room in the basement where the furnishings were the replaced or obsolete or simply no-longer-wanted objects from the rest of the house. We lay in the dark, the small windows open just below the ceiling, and I let my eyes adjust until I could make out the chest of drawers and above it, in a metal frame, a print by Auguste Renoir of a naked woman wading through a pond. Mr Klapperman had bought the print in Chicago while at a medical con-vention, and Mrs Klapperman had banished it to the basement. The Renoir woman had exquisite breasts, round and full, and the whole scene was painted in a fuzzy manner — impressionism, Howard said. It occurred to me that Andrea Rapkin's breasts were tiny in comparison but I didn't care, I was even glad, for that made her less obviously, less easily desirable.

(Howard, whose large feet at the end of the bed made two tents beneath the blanket, recounted some story about a car chase, probably from a movie.) Whenever I saw her at school I realized that she was not the perfection I had imagined the night before, but just a girl, Andrea. One day this week, for instance, the rims of her nostrils were red from hay fever. When she became bored with Mr Callaghan's drone she would write short lines in her notebook — it looked like poetry. And when I noticed such things, how it hurt, hurt violently inside my chest where there was always, even when I wasn't thinking of her, a quiet ache.

"Matt," Howard said, "you're not listening to me."

"I'm sorry. I can't help it."

"You're thinking about her."

"Let's go to sleep," I said, turning on my side.

"It's Andrea."

"I'm asleep."

"Tell me again what it's like, Matt. I've never been crazy over a girl like you are."

"It's hard to explain, maybe impossible."

"Try. *Please.*"

I sighed. "In English class Mrs Kinch told us that a writer has to find a symbol for something there isn't any words for. Maybe it's like that, maybe it's why we use the word 'love', because it just covers up what we can't express.

I don't know, sometimes I think it's not fair that I should feel this way, but then I take it back because really I'm grateful, it's kind of like a gift. And then sometimes I feel bad for Andrea. It's not like she chose for me to be thinking about her all the time. I wish I could kiss her just once. Because then she'd know how I feel, it would be like a symbol, the kind used instead of words. And if I could do that I wouldn't care about the past or the future anymore. Maybe she would love me but if she didn't at least I could feel the sorrow of that, and maybe she could be happy for the both of us. That's all I really want, just that one moment."

A shadow crossed one of the windows, probably the neighbour's fat Persian prowling the night. The watch was balanced against a glass of water on the night-table and I could hear it ticking. When Howard spoke it was in a hushed and reverential voice.

"You're a poet, Matthew, like Shakespeare or Bob Dylan. One day I hope I'll be in love like you. And to think that Andrea doesn't know." He whistled thinly. "I'll never forget this night."

I stared at Renoir's woman for a few seconds and then shut my eyes.

On Tuesday, the final day of school, classes were loud and unruly, teachers conducted games and quizzes and brought in home-baked cookies. In science we watched a film on South American killer bees. Locker doors hung open in the halls, candy wrappers and pages from notebooks drifted about discarded art projects made of papier mâché and chicken wire. I went from class to class, waiting for last period, history; beyond that I could not imagine, as if the last bell would mark the end of the world.

Despite Mr Callaghan's advance warning I was not prepared for the history test. On Sunday I had sat at my desk, doodling on the blotter or dozing with my head on my textbook. Ronny, across the hall, prepared for his summer research job. We hadn't talked since he walked out of my room and although I wanted to, I didn't know what to say.

On Sunday I hadn't been too worried about the test as there was always Monday night to cram, something I knew other kids did all the time. On Monday after school, however, I didn't go directly home but grabbed my gym bag and took two buses to reach the Y on Bathurst Street. Although we had a family membership I rarely used it, not wishing to humiliate myself in the field of athletics any more than was already demanded at school. In the locker room crowded with kids and naked old men I changed to run a few laps on the track (one shoelace recklessly undone and my shirt hanging out of my shorts) and shoot some baskets, or rather chase after rebounds. That was enough. I traded a dime for a towel from the retarded girl behind the counter and hung it around my neck the way the men did in the sauna. And then I went up to the cafeteria.

The cafeteria was a dingy room without windows, always empty except for this brief rush-hour period. The reason for my coming to the Y had been an argument in our living room on Sunday. Giving up the pretence of studying, I had descended the staircase and, obscured by the raised voices as if by smoke, was able to sit on the piano bench without being noticed. My grandmother was saying:

"A real husband would teach you what's right."

Mosey sat alone at the table, moving a chess piece across the board. He looked up, a rook in his hand.

"M-me? Oh, I don't m-mind."

"Like a loose woman."

My grandmother crossed her arms. At first I couldn't see Aunt Ida as she faced the fireplace, but when she turned I was shocked by how ravaged she looked. "This is intolerable." As she turned, the bracelets jangled on her wrist. "I can have no pleasures in this life. Like a dog, that's what I am. I don't spend money, don't go out, and now I can't have friends either —"

"Now Ida," my mother said. She came over to put her hand on Aunt Ida's forehead as if she were feeling a child's temperature. "We're all glad you have a friend like Mr Silver. Your mother is a little old fashioned, that's all."

"If only your father was alive," my grandmother said.

As Aunt Ida began to sob, my mother eased her arms around her sister-in-law. Tears choked Aunt Ida, and over my mother's shoulder, which shook with her trembling, she could only mouth a single word: "Papa . . ."

And so I stood in the open doorway of the Y cafeteria, looking for Aunt Ida. I found her, sitting at a table against the wall and laughing, with a man. She wore a mauve body-suit, her hair tied back and a matching scarf around her neck like a bandana. I could see, even from here, the mole on her breast. Mr Silver had a small round face, a thin moustache, and dimples when he smiled. He wore a toupee, not a very good one for it didn't align properly with his sideburns. This was the man whom she had met one evening at this same place and who occasionally bought her a fruit juice. He said something and Aunt Ida threw her head back, her laughter rising over the chattering at the other tables. Standing there I felt suddenly ashamed, like a spy or a Peeping Tom, and I was about to go when Aunt Ida saw me. She didn't pause in her speaking but just looked at me until I backed away.

Mr Callaghan had all the windows of the classroom closed, "So you won't have any distractions," he said. The room seemed airless and my throat felt parched even though I had just taken a drink from the water fountain outside the door. As Mr Callaghan wrote the test question on the board I gazed at Andrea, the white and blue cotton top with the thin straps leaving bare her shoulders and a square of her back. Perhaps she had forgotten to invite me to her end-of-school party and when she looked about at her guests tomorrow night would suddenly realize my absence.

"You may begin," Mr Callaghan said, stepping aside so we could read the question on the board. Andrea moaned.

"Andrea," I said.

She turned around, her brow creased from thinking about the question, making her look cross. "What do you want, Matthew?"

"Andrea, I heard that — that you were having a party and, well, if you need help or —"

"Oh, I cancelled the party."

"You did?"

"Uh-huh. I'm going to Israel for the summer, to work on a kibbutz near Haifa. And the airline flight got changed from Monday to tomorrow. Isn't it fabulous? I had to talk my parents into letting me go."

"Who's talking there?"

Andrea gave me a conspiratorial look and turned around to begin writing. Any other time that look would have been a gift of immeasurable value, but now I could see before me only the abyss of a summer without Andrea. She wouldn't even be on the same continent as me. A feeling of lethargy descended as I looked over her shoulder to read the question written on the blackboard in Mr Callaghan's immaculate hand:

*What lessons can we learn from the Second World War?*

I looked at the blank foolscap on the desk and then up again at the room, silent now except for the scratching of pens; it seemed that everyone was writing but me. Andrea was hunched over, her left shoulder leaning in. She had such beautiful hair, it made one want to touch it. Beyond the closed windows a gym class was kicking a soccer ball, and the silence made it seem like a television with the sound turned off. I unlatched the chain from my belt loop and placed the watch, its face open so that I could see the circle of roman numerals, at the corner of the desk. This watch, which had seemed to whisper a message meant especially for me, was just an object, dumb and sightless. Its ticking was not the beating of a heart, but merely the precise mechanical action of gears and springs. From outside, a shout penetrated the windows: a player had kicked the soccer ball between the goal posts. I took up my pen and began to write:

*My grandfather was a difficult man. He didn't know how to talk to children. At least he didn't know how to talk to me. But it's because of him that I'm here, going to this school. I have one brother but my grandfather had more, and sisters too. What were their names? Did he play with them? I don't know. They got burned in ovens. But knowing how someone died isn't knowing anything at all.*

When the bell sounded to end the day, voices rose up all over the school. We stayed in our seats until Mr Callaghan collected the papers, pausing at each desk to shuffle them square. Andrea turned in her seat, shaking out her hand; she had a blue smudge on the side of her palm.

"I guess I passed," she smiled.

My mother had decided that the last day of the school year called for a special celebration and so we had a patio barbecue with my father preparing his famous marinated chicken. Of course the family was invited, and although Ronny couldn't make it for dinner he promised to appear in time for the serving of my mother's strawberry flan.

My father, flamboyant in apron, manned the barbecue, a brush in one hand and a bowl of his marinade in the other. Meanwhile, my mother set the table, including a slender bottle of Carmel wine next to the arrangement of garden flowers.

From the patio I looked down the lawn to where the sprinklers, timed to coincide with the sun's decline, were starting to spurt. After a few moments they caught their rhythms and the lawn became a vision of misty arcs. "Boy, you're growing up fast," said Uncle Norman, standing at the table. "Next year it's grade nine and then high school. I bet the teachers will still remember Ronny. He was quite a student."

My father stepped back from the barbecue's heat and wiped his brow. "I'm sure Matthew doesn't want to be known as Ronny's brother," he said. "He'll do just fine with his own name."

"I never could sit still and study," said Uncle Norman. "Even now I can't read a book."

My grandmother chuckled from her deck chair. "You don't like to study because you're stupid at it."

"You hear that?" Uncle Norman threw up his hands but he grinned as if he were pleased. "Matthew, does your mother say such things about you?"

My mother was just passing behind me with a bowl of rice salad. "Never," she said, giving my arm a squeeze.

We sat down to dinner. My father wrestled the cork from the bottle of wine and we drank a toast to summer. Aunt Ida, still angry at her mother for the argument over Mr Silver and perhaps at me as well, hadn't spoken all evening. "So Matt," Uncle Norman said, reaching for the cucumbers in vinaigrette, "you've got the whole summer ahead of you. What are you going to do, get a job?"

"He has a job at home," my mother said. "Matthew's going to look after the swimming pool. It needs vacuuming and skimming and the chemicals have to be added every day."

"He can spend some time at the warehouse if he likes," my father said.

"He's too young."

Mosey, napkin tucked in his collar, examined the Carmel label. "This is v-very g-good wine."

My mother said, "Ronny would like to have some friends over for a swim on Saturday, the kids from his study group. Of course I told him that he didn't even have to ask." She passed my father the rice salad. "I want you to pick up some ice cream and soft drinks," she said.

"Of course, honey. Ida, would you like more wine?"

Aunt Ida paused so long I didn't think she would answer. "Yes, please," she said finally and looked away.

As this was my celebration I wasn't allowed to help clean up after dinner. "Your job," my mother said so that everyone could hear, "is to cheer up your aunt."

"Oh, really," Aunt Ida said with embarrassment.

"I mean it." My mother had already put her portable radio-recorder on the patio wall and now she got up to put in a cassette and turn it on. "Here, Ida, your favourite album." I recognized the music as soon as it came on, for it *was* my aunt's favourite, the musical *Hair*. My mother, moving with the music, took me by the hand to raise me from my chair. Then she took Aunt Ida's hand. "I have to make coffee, but I want to see the two of you dancing."

"Mom," I whimpered.

"Come on, it's fun."

I knew that my aunt did like to dance, although she rarely got the chance and certainly never with Mosey. But she had avoided even looking at me all evening. "Here,

Aunt Ida," I said, awkwardly taking her hand. "May I have the honour?"

Aunt Ida got up, blushing. The recorder played "This is the dawning of the age of Aquarius" as we stepped to the centre of the patio and began to dance, slowly, separately. After a while she began to look at me, and then to smile, and I could see she was enjoying the beat of the music and I realized that I was enjoying it too. We didn't speak but danced on in the deepening evening light, my grandmother and Uncle Norman and Mosey watching us. Then she began to flirt with me a little, joking about girls at school and shaking her hair out as she laughed. "You should have seen me when I was young," she said, dancing. "I was so popular! But Papa scared them off. He adored me, I was his little girl . . ."

When the music stopped my aunt kissed me and went in to help my mother. I walked into the garden, down the grass and between the ranges of the sprinklers to the end of the lawn. My running shoes and the edge of my pants became wet and the smell of grass rose up as I looked across to J. R. Henry Junior High. I wondered what I had learned this past year in a new house, at a new school, and while I was thinking I pulled the watch from my pocket, pushed the button to open the lid, and looked at the ivory face. In it I saw my grandfather in his bathing trunks, hands on hips and feet in the sand, the umbrellas and bath houses behind him. And me, a small child with a round stomach, getting scooped up in his arms, struggling free and vanishing again. I reversed it, so that I appeared from the opposite side and swooped up into his arms. Forwards, backwards, forwards, backwards. And then, my grandfather on the beach, I froze it at that one moment, me in his arms.

"Hey!"

The voice made me turn around. It was Ronny, stepping carefully on the wet grass. And beside him walked a girl. She was taller than Ronny, with loose hair, a cotton dress, wire-frame glasses. The mist from the sprinklers made them appear distant and motionless and I turned back to look at J. R. Henry and remember all the months that I had been in love with Andrea Rapkin. She would go away tomorrow and what I had to look forward to was a long summer of waiting. I would love her next year too, perhaps with just as little success, but there didn't seem anything that I could do about it.

The watch had slipped back into my pocket of its own accord. Without looking I took a couple of steps backwards and, as I turned, stepped straight into the projection of a rotating sprinkler. The line of water ran up my leg and hit me square in the face. Sputtering, I saw Ronny and the girl coming forward, smiling but not laughing. I shook the water off and, laughing so that they began to laugh too, started towards them.

*Happy Birthday*
*to Me*

"$\mathcal{N}$o, no, no," Claire said into the receiver. She trembled; tears verged.

Gene, her mother, filled a bowl with sugared almonds and licked the ends of her fingers. Light poured into the living room, turning it white on white. "What's wrong?" Gene asked pleasantly, as if nothing really could be. Claire looked at her with disbelief. She couldn't help appraising the silvery knit top with enormous shoulders, the wide crepe pants. Claire hated that Creeds look — she was as sensitive to clothes as the weather — and it only made her mother's cheery tone more exasperating.

"The shop forgot to make the cake. I can't believe it, everything's ruined."

The front door of the apartment opened, Claire could see from the living room. But it was just her sister Eve and the two kids. Michael and David raced across the room.

"Don't touch the table," Claire said. "Here, *you* talk." She handed her mother the telephone. "Hello, Judy?" Gene said. "What have they got in the shop? Uh-huh. That's what I was thinking. If you have to wait you have to wait."

A tinny roar sounded; Claire's brother-in-law had turned on the television in the bedroom. "Eve," Claire said, "can you start putting together the platters in the kitchen? The food from the deli is on the counter."

"Deli?" Eve said. "We don't let the kids touch nitrites."

"Deli is Bobby's favourite." Claire watched her sister go down the hall. "I ordered that cake six weeks ago," she said, but no one was listening. She looked down at the broadloom; not white, but *Arctic*. Everyone had told her she was crazy, the whiteness would never last. But it looked brilliant. She could see it through the mitred-glass top of the coffee table as if through a magnifying glass. When people saw it they gasped. The whole room was light, the sofa (with a thread of turquoise), the corner chairs with their lacquered arms, the porcelain lamps and Japanese shades. On the glass table, in a crystal bowl, blood-red orchid blossoms. The same colour as Claire's lipstick.

The man at the bakery had assured her the cake would be ready. She'd like to bang a cake-knife against his head. Eve was crashing around in the kitchen, Claire hoped she wouldn't make a mess. She could be so sloppy. "Tell them to keep us informed," Claire said to her mother who was saying goodbye on the receiver. She turned her rings easily around her finger. The diamond was always catching on things. If she had lost weight again it was because of arranging this party.

"Michael, David, come here," she called. The stomping of feet and then the two boys skidding in from the hall, Michael first as always. "You two have a job to do." She kneeled down to them. "Think you can handle it?"

"What is it?" said Michael.

"Blowing up balloons."

"All right!"

"They're in the bedroom, three packages on the dresser. "But listen —" she grabbed onto their shirt-tails — "you have to keep them in the bedroom. Otherwise they'll give the surprise away when Bobby gets here."

They took off. As Claire stood up she saw Lionel leaning in the arch that defined the living and dining rooms. He didn't look like Bobby's brother, he was too dark and weasel-thin. Arms folded across his "Festival des Films du Monde" T-shirt, jeans rolled at the bottom, Red Converse runners. His smile made her nervous, as if he were laughing at her. "It was good of you to come into town," she said. That sounded too prissy; his smile expanded.

"What are brothers for?" he said. "I'm going down the street for cigarettes." His voice drawled, like early Brando. She detested smoking but couldn't stop herself from nodding. He grinned even more and loped by her.

At the door he came up against Norman Salinsky, stooping to avoid knocking his head and holding the baby in one hand as if it were a football. "Hey, if it isn't Lionel Barrymore," Norman said. "Later," Lionel mumbled and was out the door. "What's gotten into him?" Norman's voice boomed. It always boomed.

"He thinks you're making fun of him," said Marla, coming up behind and lugging with two hands an enormous carry-bag.

"People are so touchy. Claire!" He held up the bundle. "Look what I've got."

Claire came over and kissed the baby's cheek. "Hello, Monica, sweetie. Aren't you adorable."

"We've brought half of Shoppers Drug Mart with us," Marla said.

"Yeah, our motto is never travel light. Ha! Are we the first?" he asked, stepping into the living room and holding Monica at a forty-five degree angle towards the floor.

"Oh, be careful," said Claire.

"Don't worry," Marla said. "She loves it. You have to get used to watching Norman with Monica, it's a little terrifying at first."

"So Bobby's hitting the big three-o," Norman said. "Is that jerk going to be surprised. I can't wait to see the look on his face when he comes in. In public school we used to eat dog biscuits together."

"We know," said Marla, easing Monica from his grasp. "Claire dear, can I use the kitchen to fix a bottle? The breast-feeding is *finito*, thank God."

"You guys are so lucky," Claire said. "She's beautiful. And all that hair."

"Hey, having kids is a trend these days," Norman said. "Like sushi. It isn't hard to make one. I'll explain it to Bobby."

"My husband thinks he's David Letterman. Claire, the place looks terrific. I love the rug under the dining-room table — is it Mexican? This is a perfect doll's house."

"Before you, Bobby lived like a pig," Norman said.

"He has a lot of other things to think about," Claire said. "He gets a little careless."

"That's one way to describe it."

"Marla, I'll come with you."

"Good, because I want to hear how the job's going —"

Norman tilted one side of his glasses with the palm of his hand (but they fell back; the temple was bent) and ambled towards the bay window. "Bobby, Bobby," he said aloud and slouched onto the sofa and started to hum. A lot of noise in the kitchen — he knew to stay clear. Oldest buddies. At Bobby's kitchen table Mrs Gross used to serve them tuna sandwiches and glasses of milk. Once they made a bomb and blew up a toilet, causing a flood. Bobby didn't call him goof-ball or pecker-legs or any of the other schoolyard names. Bobby never even *heard* them. Oldest buddies.

Norman looked up at the man with the beard coming in from the hall, Eve's husband, the accountant.

"Anything to drink?" he said.

"I don't think the bar's open yet," Norman answered.

"Jesus."

He turned around. Claire came in from the dining room with Marla, who was holding the bottle to Monica. "It was going to be the most elegant cake," Claire was saying. "Mocha, with calligraphy lettering. Now I don't know what we're getting."

Claire's father, Meyer, came up behind them wearing a calico apron. "Claire," he said. "Your mother's worried that we won't have enough pastrami. She's sending me out on a deli raid."

He was shorter than his daughter, peppery-haired and still handsome to her friends. Claire said, "Daddy, you can't leave now."

"It's all right, Bobby's not supposed to arrive for almost an hour."

"What if he leaves early?"

"Our Bobby?"

"Hey," Norman said, rising from the sofa. "We could set up a look-out system. With walkie-talkies."

"I've got a better idea," chuckled Meyer. "A rented helicopter could survey —"

"Stop it!"

Claire had stamped her foot. The men looked down at the broadloom. She smiled and put a hand on each of them; when she touched men they wanted to serve her. Meyer looked at his daughter. She'd always been petite but she looked too thin. Took everything so seriously. But he couldn't advise her, the words faded to a stammer. Her mother was better at it and really, women were more sensitive, men just made a mess of things. Perhaps Bobby helped her to have more fun. He seemed a nice enough fellow, but he was always thinking about something else. Still, he was the only one who ever asked Meyer about his fishing. How the various sorts of reels worked or Meyer's own theory of fly-sewing. If this party weren't on (not that he minded, if it pleased Claire) he would have been up in Muskoka right now, the water rushing against the tops of his waders, stretching back his rod —

"There's no need for helicopters," Claire said. "Bobby's going to phone before he leaves. I reminded him three times."

"You should have reminded him four. Ha!" Norman barked, but Marla gave him a look. Monica sucked evenly and stared at the ceiling.

"I still have so much to do," Claire said with a start. A knock on the door made them turn their heads.

"The guests," Meyer said and, reaching back, cast an invisible fly over the coffee table.

He ought not to be looking at the pile of travel brochures, but he kept on dropping one after another onto the desk as if he were dealing cards — Jamaica, Puerto Rico, Club Med. Photographs of cabana bars and bronzed women trailing shirts on deserted beaches. He'd looked at them several times without reading a word. Raising his eyes to the window he saw the glinting Royal Bank Plaza and a tiny man on a stage, cleaning windows. A precarious, existential job; he might like it himself, swish swish with the wiper, the eternal cleaning of windows. But he was here — he! — in his own office, on a Sunday, and wearing a sweatshirt with holes in it for God's sake. Men in their forties liked to shake his hand. They paid him; he wanted to laugh.

The file on his desk. When he looked down at the columns of figures, the Xeroxed floorplans, he drew a blank. And then it came back to him, like film being scraped off a window, and he slipped into his swivel chair and ran his finger across a demographics chart. Where was the breakdown of start-up costs? Somehow he would have to come to a decision. Three or four hundred thousand would get spent because of what he said. He blinked. The responsibility didn't move him at all. He was indifferent. *I am indifferent.* The thought excited him. His heart skipped.

Puerto Rico, Nassau . . . Claire liked a clean hotel, she was fussy about things like that. A phobia about insects. As a kid he'd kept them in jars, monarch caterpillars spinning chrysalides, a praying mantis that struck at his finger and flared its wings. He would forget them in the garage or basement and find the jars months later, dry shells rattling on the bottoms. Why did they have to make holiday plans now when they weren't going until bloody Christmas? A job took away spontaneity. Mexico, the Canary Islands . . .

"Excuse me, Robert. Would you like a coffee?"

In the doorway stood what's-her-name, Livesay's secretary. He was terrible with names; Claire always got embarrassed. A pretty woman. "Are you chained in here too?" he said.

"Afraid so. That expansion report has to be ready for the morning. Would you like some?"

"Sorry?"

"Coffee."

Caffeine was the worst thing for him, the shrink had told him to stay off it, not that doctors knew anything. "Sure. Unless we've got some of that mineral water in the fridge."

"I'll check," she smiled and turned around.

"You're a saint — Cindy," he called, her name suddenly appearing. She had a nice walk. He leaned back in his chair and pulled open, shut, and open again the desk drawer. Paper clips, calculator, one of those claw things for removing staples. He used to visit his father's office where he'd been allowed to choose one item from the stationary closet to take home. The secretaries had ruffled his hair; he liked that. They wore short skirts. That was what he felt like now, a kid in his dad's office. He would have been happy shooting elastic bands at the flourescent light fixtures.

On the desk stood two photographs in plexiglass frames, one of Claire on their wedding day, white silk dress, sprig of something-or-other in her hair. He ought to call her up right now and say he loved her. No, he'd wait until he got home. The other photograph was of him, taken with the delay on his Nikon, standing on Masada. Unbearably hot, he'd been dizzy from dehydration, but it was the greatest moment of his life. Maybe moments of revelation were always solitary. He looked at Claire.

"One Perrier coming up," said Cindy. She put the bottle and glass next to the file. "I'll be in the Xerox room if you need me."

"Sounds like a song title." She laughed. He said, "My report's supposed to go into that kit you're making up."

"I don't mind sticking around until you're done."

She smiled again but it annoyed him this time and he watched her go. What the hell did she want from him? "Concentrate," he said aloud and stared down at the file. Of the twelve possible sites, he had whittled them down to three. He was, somehow, good at this. If he sat long enough, his head would clear and the answer would suspend itself before him, like a diamond in a murky ocean. That made him feel invincible.

One site meant a zoning hassle, not worth it when Livesay was paranoid about dealing with city departments. The man positively foamed at the mouth over them, wanted Bobby to share in the hate sessions, like in *1984*. Take it easy, Bobby had said, they're just asserting their reality, you know?

That left two sites. Maybe he ought to toss a coin.

Something was special about this day, but he couldn't remember what. There was pleasure in removing the papers of the discarded site from the file: simplify, simplify. The ten months he'd been here was the longest he'd ever done anything. Claire was proud of him and that was worth something. She who'd been a pharmacist in the same doctor's building for four years. She had hunted for the apartment, paid the key money, chosen the furniture. All he'd done was propose to her, the night at the Exhibition when they'd become separated from Mark and Linda and after Claire had become sick on the Ferris wheel. The rain had suddenly poured down and they had gone into the agriculture building to get dry. Afterwards she'd put her head against his shoulder and wept while he stared down at the world's smallest pony.

"Cindy!"

She was passing his door with an armful of spiral-bound books. "Yes, Robert?"

Only here did they call him that, Robert; it made him want to giggle or run, as if he were playing grown-up. "I need the Donwoods lease."

"You got it."

"You know what, Cindy?"

"What, Robert?"

"Today's my birthday."

∽

If everything were not perfect then it was a failure. But it might still be perfect. A candlestick in each hand, Claire stopped under the arch to watch her mother on the telephone receiving the latest cake update from Judy. But she couldn't hear over the buzz; the guests occupied the sofa, the chairs, leaned in the hall, toured the apartment, and cooed their admiration. Eve had been assigned to the kitchen to keep them from drifting in and picking at the platters — the food was for after Bobby's arrival. Claire could hear Bobby's name here and there, like helium balloons rising towards the ceiling. She smiled, had her cheek kissed, laughed at a joke she couldn't take in. All this was her doing. She had made their lives converge, made them laugh, made them wear khaki shorts. She wanted to leap onto the dining-room table and make a deep and graceful curtsy. A roar rose from down the hall and went dead. Her brother-in-law strolled into the living room, tipping back an Upper Canada that he had sneaked from the refrigerator. "What was that?" someone asked. "Ti-Cats," he said, wiping his chin. "Picked off an end pass. Makes me sick."

"They ought to fold the whole league," Mark Eisenberg said, as he came in the front door carrying a bottle of champagne. Behind him was Linda and, as usual, Arlene, who had begged a lift. Mark heard his own voice over the crowd with a strange hollow clarity. He shook several hands as he made his way through the living room. "The box business is terrific. No, still engaged. That's right, Bobby and Claire beat us to it. What nerve, eh?" Linda was still behind him, but Arlene had disappeared somewhere. They reached the arch and took turns kissing Claire, who had a bowl of cut fruit in her arms.

"You look great," Linda said. "And you've done an incredible job with the party."

"I just want it to work out."

"If I know Bobby, he'll be the most surprised birthday boy on the planet," Mark said.

"Did he say anything when you played racquetball on Thursday?"

"Not a thing."

"See that?" Linda pushed up Mark's hair. "He hit himself with the racquet. Could have gotten his eye."

"I feel a little faint," Claire said.

"Here, sit down." Linda pulled out a dining-room chair. "You're working too hard. We've brought a bottle of champagne."

"That's so sweet. Maybe Mark could put it in the refrigerator for me."

"Glad to do my bit. Whoa —"

A small boy grabbed him about the legs and then

dashed off again. He left Linda and Claire and went into the dining room where two women he didn't know were admiring the table. That lucky Bobby; Claire had actually found an apartment with a deck above a garden. The dining room had a sliding glass door fitted with vertical blinds. Linda had been right: Claire was good for Bobby. The bottle heavy in his hands, he stepped into the kitchen. And froze. Claire's father — Meyer, as he insisted on being called — tapping a container of potato salad into a serving dish. Mark stepped back and stood against the wall. Mr Stromm was sure to grasp Mark by the shirt sleeve and *engage* him. Mr Stromm always said he liked to get the opinion of "young people," especially someone with first-hand knowledge. What knowledge? Mr Stromm couldn't understand: Mark didn't care about sanctions, about Bishop Tutu, or the emigration of liberal whites. He had been just eleven when they left, a kid. He didn't mourn for the servants or the ranch or anything else.

He pressed the champagne bottle against his chest. He wasn't political and, besides, talking about South Africa was a game he couldn't win, having committed the error of being born there. Sometimes, meeting someone new, he could feel the revulsion at the accent he had almost convinced himself he no longer possessed. He was Canadian, he wanted to shout, a fan of the dismal Maple Leafs, with paperbacks by Alice Munro on the dresser. His childhood was a forgotten landscape. Only once every year or so, during a thunderstorm, did he dream of the small dark boy who had been the housekeeper's son.

Mr Stromm had gone out the other doorway into

the hall and Mark slipped into the kitchen and put the champagne on the pink-top 1950s table in immaculate condition. What Mark *did* want to talk about was software. For stock reordering, distribution efficiency. Almost nobody understood what he did at the company, including Linda. Bobby understood. When Mark had described his new program idea for multiple-warehouse inventory control, Bobby anticipated the flaws. He got excited. Instantly called for them to form a partnership, rent office space, start a marketing plan. Mark had got so worked up that he had spent half the night at his desk. But the next week Bobby had forgotten. When Mark had been on the verge of quitting his job! He had to laugh, just thinking about it.

"Mark, just the man I want to see."

Mr Stromm's voice. There was no getting away, so Mark turned, smiling. "I didn't see you there, Mr Stromm."

"Please, call me Meyer. I've got a very strong opinion on the arrest of those journalists." Mark felt a tug; Mr Stromm had pinched his shirt sleeve.

In the living room, the boys clung to their mother's legs. Eve and Claire stood by the telephone while Gene received another cake report. "Mom," Michael said, "Aunt Claire told us to blow up every last balloon, but we're dizzy."

Claire paled. "Oh no, I never —"

"Good news," her mother said over the receiver. "They're onto the lettering."

The noise from the living room had grown intolerable. It pressed on Arlene Marks like hands against her ears and only eased when she closed the bedroom door behind her. The room was dark and cool. Her eyes adjusted; she saw the double bed afloat in languidly waving balloons. Women's things on the night-table. Arlene wanted to lie down, sleep even, miss the entire party. She sat down on the edge of the bed and a few balloons tumbled.

This was their bedroom, Claire's and Bobby's, but it felt like hers, not his. On the dresser were piled gifts and there were more, she saw now, on the floor. She hadn't brought a gift on principle, although no one would mind; they expected that sort of thing from her. She could anticipate the unwrapping, Bobby on the carpet in the middle of the living room with paper and ribbon strewn about and the rest of them applauding, like a birthday party for a six-year-old. What she had really been afraid of was buying something so ridiculously extravagant that when he came to open it she would have rushed from the room.

"Bobby." She whispered it, to hear the sound of his name in his — their — bedroom. The room seemed too chaste. She scratched at her nose, it never stopped peeling in the sun. She had come straight from Harbourfront where she taught children to sail. *I like kids, they eat up experience*; that's what she told people. Before that she had been away seven months, working as a bartender in Australia. Of course she'd missed the wedding, but that didn't look odd when she had been away for half of the last six years, guiding tours in Banff, making beds on cruise ships, anything to be outdoors. It was Bobby she wrote to most regularly, laborious descriptions of skin diving on coral reefs and the price of local wine — no doubt he yawned his way through them. His replies, care of American Express, arrived less frequently, scrawled, rambling, and funny. Sometimes he wrote: Are you happy?

She lowered herself across the bed, balloons whisking from beneath her. She was staying with her parents now, as she always did when she came back home to save money for the next trip. That Arlene, people said and shook their heads. She knew what they thought. God, she hated these gatherings. In the living room they were going on and on about the price of houses: wasn't it shocking, if you didn't buy now you'd never get on the ladder. Bobby said that she was the only true existentialist he knew. He said she was courageous.

She waved her arms, like making an angel in the snow, and balloons went careening. Two summers ago she had lived for three months on a tiny island near Corfu, had to pay a man in a tin boat to take her there. The wooden shack had a rotten smell so she slept on the beach. One day she had seen a figure walking towards her on the sand, carrying a raincoat and a bag. She had recognized Bobby before she could see his face. Out of the blue, he had simply booked a plane ticket and come. Stayed with her for ten days. She closed her eyes. No one else ever knew, they thought he had gone to Algonquin Park. Every morning they had swam in the Adriatic, just after light. He had held her and asked her: Are you happy, Arlene?

The door opened. She sat up. Lionel stood in the rectangle of light, squinting into the room. He switched on the light and, seeing her blink, gave her his knowing smile.

"What's up, Arlene?" he asked. "Basking in the sanctity of the marriage bed?"

"Piss off, Lionel." She strode past him out of the room. He stood there watching her go down the hall. He shouldn't have said that, Arlene was all right. Why did he? She was the only one of his brother's friends he liked. "Damn," he said and turned out the light.

Arthur Yates saw Arlene come in from the hall and tried to call her, but there were too many people in the way and it would have been undignified to shout. He hadn't seen Arlene since she came back from picking grapes in France or somewhere. He looked down and saw his reflection in the coffee table, but too faint to tell how he looked. He saw the world through Italian sunglasses with violet lenses. Made it look like a damn underground film.

"Mrs Stromm." He kissed Claire's mother on her downy cheek. She looked startled and then laughed, flattered. "You look terrific," he said. "Must be one of those fitness programs. Pritikin, right? No? You're putting me on." She had to lean forward to hear his close, rasping voice. Hadn't he heard? The bakery had lost the order for the cake. "That's an outrage," he said. "Don't they know how important this party is?"

Mrs Stromm excused herself and headed for the kitchen. Arthur tapped his espadrille-clad foot; he hated standing alone at a party, even for a minute; people thought you had no friends. He ought to hand out some cards — you never knew where business would turn up. This morning he'd been offered twelve thousand Taiwanese toothbrushes and a gross of factory-second snowboots, if only he could come up with the cash by tomorrow. That Bobby, how he lucked into a sixty-grand job he would never know. When all Arthur had was a rented office on Bathurst Street surrounded by Hassidic diamond merchants.

He had been giving Bobby advice to go into business since undergrad and then suddenly Bobby leapfrogged over all of them —

At last, someone to talk to. "Mark Eisenberg," he said and was already stretching out a hand. "You look good, absolutely terrific."

"Arthur, I always dress like a bum compared to you. That's quite a look."

"You like it?" True, he had good taste: pleated trousers rolled above bare ankles, silk blouse, a team jacket of chamois leather. "I go to this Italian tailor on Dufferin, does magnificent work. You give him my name and he'll treat you like royalty."

"I was just looking at Bobby's photographs. Claire's put them up."

"She has?" said Arlene, who was just passing. The three turned to the row of frames suspended museum-like above the sofa. Each a silvery image of a pair of feet — on pavement, grass, linoleum squares.

"I don't know why he stopped," Mark said. "These are good. They're so weirdly expressive."

"Hmm," said Arlene. She was looking at a pair of tanned and slender feet sunk into the Mediterranean sand. *Her* feet.

"Okay, but where does it get him?" said Arthur. Bobby had once gone on and on about the honesty of naked feet, or some such crap. It's not honesty you need to learn, Arthur had told him, it's dishonesty —

"Don't they look nice?" Claire said. She was just

passing with an armful of gifts. "Bobby would have let them sit in a box forever."

"Maybe he'll get inspired to take more," Mark said. "He was always mumbling about it."

"I hope so." But she didn't hope so. She had framed them so that he wouldn't take it up again, so that the photographs would hang there, beautiful and embalmed. It worked too; after the first couple of days Bobby didn't look at them again.

"Look out —"

They turned. David, Eve's youngest boy, had let a glass of Coke slip from his hand. The guests parted and stared down at the sepia arc spreading into the Arctic broadloom.

David started to cry. Claire grabbed a handful of napkins. "Don't worry," Norman Salinsky said, "that's what parties are for."

⁓

*Studies show that a steadily growing number of consumers are coming to accept the concept of higher-priced, specialty-flavoured popcorn as a gourmet item. Nevertheless, a substantial population still holds to the archaic notion that popcorn belongs only in movie theatres. While part of our mandate must be to overcome consumer indifference, we can not do so at the expense of maximum profitability . . .*

He leaned back to read his words on the screen. Like an artist admiring his canvas. He found the sort of language that set off vigorous nods of assent around the boardroom table surprisingly easy to manufacture, he could go on for pages or until he grew bored. Only he couldn't make a decision about which of the two remaining sites to recommend, and he paused to prop his feet on the edge of the desk and lean back with his head resting on his hands. The desk — Claire would go crazy — was a chaos of papers, blueprints, memos, but otherwise he couldn't think. Where had he buried his *Manchester Guardian Weekly*? Lately he'd found himself obsessed with the news and read three papers a day, sometimes missed his stop on the subway. This week he'd been fascinated with a certain kickback scandal in Delhi, and he was following scrupulously the European cricket semi-finals, even though the scores were as hard to decipher as a secret wartime code.

Why hadn't he realized it before? He swung down his feet and landed them with a thump beneath his desk. The company didn't even realize that it was on the verge of deciding its future course. The board believed that the next expansion phase depended on the relative profit projections of franchise versus company ownership. But the reports, the breakfast-meeting arguments, they all circled around one unspoken question: which were the best locations, malls, or street-sites? He laughed out loud. The company was crying for a definitive statement, firm and authoritative. His own choice was easy: he liked streets better than malls. Streets were more alive, more real. Malls were commercial Disneylands, stage sets. In malls there was no individualism, no genuine free will. Besides, malls confused his sense of direction and left him nauseous. But the company? The best strategy would be to create a graph; the boardroom loved graphics that justified the computer system. He grabbed some papers — walking traffic statistics, demographics. A few taps on the keyboard and he had the coloured bars going up like toy skyscrapers.

But his eye caught the corner of the *Guardian*, buried beneath some folders. He pulled it out, leisurely draped it across the desk, and read a headline beneath the fold. "Israeli Soldier Panics, Shoots Palestinian Youth." He drew in his breath and shut his eyes. He didn't know what he felt. Only that he remembered long tables, dawn outside the window and the buzz of voices, bowls of fruit for breakfast. After the summer on the kibbutz he had wanted to emigrate. *Aliyah.* Back home he had dragged his parents to Shabbat services. His mother had pleaded: in Israel they made everyone go into the army. He asked them to call him Rachmael, his Hebrew name. So why didn't he go? He just didn't. Let the date on the plane ticket pass, spent three weeks in pyjamas lying on the sofa watching *Star Trek*.

He yawned. Claire was expecting him home, she'd made dinner reservations at some Yorkville restaurant. Turning thirty: it was something of a surprise.

In the Israeli army he would have learned to assemble a gun in the dark.

⁂

"Now remember," Claire said. She didn't like speaking to an audience; her voice went shrill. She ran her fingers up the loop of pearls, one of Bobby's impulsive gifts.

Otherwise she had dressed as plain as could be — a white cotton top, linen trousers, suede loafers. It was stupid, how she had rehearsed these words about not letting Bobby suspect anything; but she had, over and over.

"That's why everybody is going to wait on the deck. He might call at any time and we don't want a last-minute panic. After he comes into the apartment I'll open the sliding door and you'll all stream into the room."

Norman said, "How come we don't just wait inside and surprise him when he comes in?"

"Because if he's at all suspicious he'll expect that. And he might hear you. This way when he sees the empty apartment he'll be disarmed. And besides, I want it to be different."

"What do we do as we're coming in from the deck?" Amy West asked. "Do we sing 'Happy Birthday'?"

"Yes, *yes*." Claire put her palm to her forehead. She had forgotten that.

Arlene thought Claire sounded a little frantic. She filed past Claire who was holding the handle of the sliding door, smiling like the Queen, and went onto the deck. It was raised above the garden and the first guests had lined up along the rail to view the backyards of the houses in the next street. As the last few came through the doors Arlene felt herself pressed on all sides, her face nearly touching someone's shoulder. She wouldn't doubt if Claire had used a mathematical formula, depending on estimated waist-sizes, to form the guest list. The sliding door shut with a whomp and they all went silent.

"Baa, baa."

It was Lionel, Bobby's brother. They all laughed. They found it funny, being crammed on this deck. Someone began talking about a bicycle trip through France. Marla let Linda take the baby, in sweater and sunbonnet, onto her shoulder. Lionel leaned against the apartment brick and pretended to pant under the declining sun. He pulled the band from his ponytail and shook loose his hair. Why had he bothered to come back from Montreal for this? Because he thought they would take notice — after all he'd been gone five months — but as usual everybody was making a fuss about Bobby. When it was Lionel who had been on St. Denis and Sherbrooke and had climbed to the cross at two in the morning. Who had slept in the beds of *two* French-speaking women. Who was studying with Anna Klaj! Every moment he had doubted, doubted everything, but at least had thought that somehow they were all wondering about him. Sometimes he even felt that they were watching him. But they weren't, he saw that now, not even Bobby, who had hardly noticed that he'd left —

"Lionel, how's it going?"

Norman again, one of Bobby's high-school clowns.

"You still doing the acting thing?" Norman said.

"Still doing it, Norm."

"Whatever happened to that, you know, that acting group you were going to form?"

"Didn't work out."

"No?"

"No, I've moved on from there. Right now I'm taking an advanced acting workshop in Montreal with an incredible teacher. German."

"Montreal, eh? I hear it's a pretty sophisticated town these days."

At least this was something. Lionel raised his voice. "Norman, compared to Montreal, Toronto is a cemetery. A giant bank. Montreal is loose, it has style, it's sexy. People there know how to live. And you don't have to apologize for being an artist. They honour you. Being born in Toronto was an accident, a mistake of fate, or maybe I was robbed from a cradle. In Montreal I've found my milieu. I'm living in cafés and theatres. It's a completely different existence."

Someone's elbow stuck Norman in the back. He lowered his eyes at Lionel and then slowly rolled them. "Yeah?" he said. "So how are the Chinese restaurants?"

The baby woke and started to cry. Marla took her back from Linda to rock and kiss her, but the mewls turned to gasping hiccups and her face deepened to plum. "Is she okay?" Norman said, trying to see over heads. "What are you doing to her?"

"I'm torturing her, what do you think I'm doing? She needs another bottle. But I don't want to spoil Claire's plan."

"You can go in the bedroom," Linda said.

"That's an idea." Marla banged with one hand on the sliding door. A few moments later it opened a crack. Marla spoke quietly and then the door opened wider, she slipped in with the baby, and it shut again.

"I'm getting hungry," someone said.

"And it's hot — I'm sweating."

Lionel said, "Is this elevator going up?" No one laughed; it wasn't funny anymore.

"Where the hell's Bobby?"

Steven and Amy West were arguing, but gently. Her hands rested on the roundness beneath her jumpsuit. Steven was most annoying when he worried over her, but she still refused to go inside and upset Claire. "I feel fine," Amy said. He was embarrassing her in front of Arthur Yates, who had hung his sunglasses from the open front of his shirt.

"Can I touch?" Arthur said.

"Sure, go ahead," Steven grinned. Amy just looked at him. Arthur put his hand lightly on her belly. Well, it felt nice. "Beautiful," said Arthur.

Mark Eisenberg squeezed up to them. "Steven, I hear you and Bobby used to play hockey together."

"Just street hockey, after his family moved into the neighbourhood. Listen to this. One Sunday we played against the team from the apartments. That's what we called those kids, 'The Apartments,' like they were thugs because they didn't live in houses. Truth is, we were afraid of them. But they challenged us and we wanted to win. A very cold day, the air hurt your lungs when you ran. It was a tough game, lots of illegal checks, slashing, grabbing at the ball. They would score and then we would score —"

"Is there a short version to this story?" Amy said. "I'm due in seven weeks."

"You have to get the flavour. So it's tied three-all and in a few minutes everybody has to go home for supper. I take a faceoff, win it for once in my life, and drop the ball back to Kenny Schneiderman. Kenny makes a long pass up the road and hits guess who right on his blade."

"Bobby," Mark said.

"Right. Bobby's got a breakaway up the side, there isn't a single body between him and the goalie. I'm praying he doesn't lose the ball between his feet. But he doesn't, he moves like a ballerina, dekes the goalie, and lifts the ball up into the net. Instant mayhem. We're yelping like we've just won the Stanley Cup."

"That's incredible," said Mark.

"Wait, I'm not finished. Bobby waves his hands in the air. No goal, he says, the ball hit the crossbar. Jesus, even the goalie thought it was in. The game ends in a tie. And Bobby goes around shaking hands with the other team's players."

"That's so sweet," said Amy.

Sweet? Steven had wanted to strangle Bobby. The next time they played the apartments they got creamed.

Sweet? Arthur gave his rasping laugh. Bobby was a poor S.O.B., no instinct for the kill. He would never learn not to give up an advantage.

Sweet? Mark squinted as the sun slipped between two houses. In Johannesburg he had played rugger. Yes, it was sweet. He wished he had played hockey.

∽

The ball of paper arced over the desk, touched the rim of the can, and spun out. "No points," Bobby said. The Perrier bottle was empty; he put the rim to his lips and blew a note. He had the report written, the arguments and statistics — everything but the final decision on the site. It was possible that his choice would be wrong, for any number of reasons. Cosmic reasons. No matter. He waited for inspiration.

The inspiration didn't come.

Waiting was boring, although he noticed a slight erection in his shorts. Ignoring it, he got one knee up on his desk so that he could look out the window and see the rising skeleton of the dome stadium. The sun had turned it orange and hard to look at. For months he had used a small pair of binoculars from his desk to view the men clinging to the girders. Nothing was more pleasant than the sight of men building something; he could spend whole days that way. When he was nine he had once passed an afternoon watching workmen pour concrete and then smooth it into a sidewalk. When he had got home his mother stood sobbing on the front porch beside a policeman. He remembered looking up at her in surprise from the bottom of the steps.

Still no inspiration.

He opened the desk drawer and fished around, pulling out a blank sheet of paper. Then folded it into an airplane. His own design, it demanded precise angles and even pressure of the thumbnail.

"Excuse me, Robert, I was wondering if you had that report to be Xeroxed?"

"Not quite ready," he said, sitting up. She looked rather impatient to leave and had her purse under her arm. Her name was Carla, no, Sheila? Would he like to sleep with her? Claire would get upset and it wasn't as if one could forget mentioning that sort of thing. He had once written a paper in university on the mind/body problem —

"What if you left it for me to do first thing in the morning?" she said.

"Excellent idea. I'll put it right on your desk."

"Are you going on the company boat cruise next weekend?" she said. "It's always a lot of fun."

"I haven't thought about it. Do you want me to?"

But he wasn't listening to her answer, he was trying to remember where Claire had made the reservation for dinner. He didn't feel any thirty-year crisis coming on. In fact, he felt quite content, sitting in his swivel chair, in his own office. He could sit here all evening, or at least until he came up with a final paragraph. What he had to do was tap into the other side — the creative as opposed to the analytical side — of his brain. He'd read about that in an issue of *Science* before his subscription lapsed.

"Yes, see you tomorrow." She had a nice behind, pear-shaped. Maybe if he subscribed again he could get one of those free gifts, an electronic phone dialer or a pocket star-chart. There was nothing he liked better than getting a package in the mail. There! The paper airplane sailed through the doorway.

༄

"Where *is* he?"

Claire tapped the coffee table with her nails, immaculately filed and painted the palest rose. She had to say it quietly or she might shriek it, down on her knees, her nails drawing blood from her arms. Bobby was an hour and a half late.

"I'm sure he'll call any minute. He's never been on time, not even for the wedding." Her mother's voice soft and cool as a salve, as when Claire the child had awoken from sleep in terror. There had been a recurring dream, Claire in a scarlet dress, trying to dance on a glass floor that fell away beneath her.

"Where is he?" she said again.

"We just have to be patient. Can't you give him a call?"

"The switchboard's shut down on Sunday. He's going to ruin everything. I wanted him to feel that every day of the rest of his life was going to be special."

"He *will* feel it, Claire. You're all hot" — Gene put her hand against Claire's forehead. "You're going to make yourself sick. Come and have a cold drink."

The front door swung open, they could see it from the living room. Harold Gross, Bobby's father, walking backwards with one end of a large bakery box in his hands. He always looked like a walrus to Claire. A red-faced walrus. At the other end of the box, smiling, Judy Gross.

"Where's the birthday boy?" Judy sung.

"Not quite here yet," Gene said. "Bring the cake into the kitchen. We've made a space in the fridge."

"Wait, I want to see it," Claire said.

Meyer came in from the kitchen. "Harold," he called, "what took you so long?"

"Very amusing," Harold said. The bakery box rubbed against his stomach. Below his shorts he wore argyle socks and white Florsheims. Meyer directed them towards the coffee table as if he were bringing down a 747. As they lowered the box Judy said, "It was the best we could do." Harold exhaled loudly, meaning that she should keep quiet. She was always apologizing, it drove him round the bend. Besides, it wasn't their fault even though they did have to pay for it by enduring two hours of women's squabbles over poppyseed bagels and *challahs*. It was the bakery's fault or Claire's or Bobby's or maybe all of them. Judy had been making excuses for Bobby since he was four. Sure, he was making decent money now, but a dollar still meant nothing to that kid and anyway, how long would it last? Bobby wouldn't quit, he didn't have the drive for that, he'd just get sloppy and incompetent until they would have to fire him. Then he would talk about life being meaningless or some other bull, and quote one of his Nazi philosophers — that was the great benefit of an arts education. And Lionel was no better, an actor yet, hanging around with slutty girls and homos. That was the result of giving his children the best. And the worst was they wouldn't listen to their father, not one word, as if in his whole life he could have learned nothing worth imparting. Not even a single story about when he was a young man, they wouldn't listen even out of sympathy, just to let him tell it.

Claire lifted the lid of the bakery box. They stared down at a pink-frosted, six-pointed star. It read HAPPY BIRTHDAY BOB.

"A Star of David?" said Gene.

"It was meant for a Bar Mitzvah," Judy said. "They had it in the freezer. The girl tried to write 'Bobby' but she ran out of icing. She was just weekend help."

They all looked down at the cake. Meyer had never liked Harold. The man, as he told Gene after their first meeting, was a blowhard. Harold had made their dinner reservation, ordered the wine, and insisted on picking up the cheque with a flourish of his Gold Card. But Meyer never liked to make trouble, didn't he pride himself on getting along with everybody? The most important thing was for Claire to be happy.

But here, looking at the cake, he couldn't resist.

"I hope Bob will like it," Meyer said.

"My son's name is not Bob," Harold said. "We've never called him that. It's Bobby."

"But it says 'Bob' right there."

"I don't care what the frigging cake says. His name's Bobby."

"It doesn't matter, dear," said Judy.

"Of course it matters. The man can call his son-in-law by the right name."

"Of course," said Meyer. "I just thought you would have done better, with the cake I mean."

"I can't believe what I'm hearing." Harold's voice cracked. "I gave that shopgirl hell, she was in tears. It's a miracle that we got this. You should be down on your knees thanking us."

"Us? Bob is your son."

"Bobby!"

"And we do thank you. Even Harold Gross can't do the impossible. I'm sure you at least got a discount."

"A discount? Now I'm speechless. You want to know what I think of that cake? I'll show you what —"

Claire placed her hands over the box. "Would you all please wait on the deck," she said. "Mother and I will put the cake in the fridge. Bobby's going to call any minute."

"I don't want to wait on the deck," Harold said.

"We're doing what Claire says." Judy took him by the arm. When the door slid open they were surprised by the faces staring at them, silent and unsmiling.

"My son is an idiot," Harold said.

∽

When he was a child he had always had a birthday party in the backyard, around card tables decorated with crepe paper. His mother baked the cake and stuck Smarties into the icing to make his name. His father always wore the silliest hat and made him laugh. The neighbourhood kids ran around the backyard, "like Indians" his mother would say, and Lionel would stand beside him, in awe of his brother's new age. His favourite gifts had been a model called "The Human Body" and books by Dr Seuss; *Horton Hears a Who* had shaken his earliest metaphysical beliefs. At about five o'clock the mothers would start to arrive to drag their kids home and then the house would go quiet, only the sound of his mother at the kitchen sink and his father at the television, and he and Lionel would stand among the wrappings and the gifts, not knowing what to do.

What he ought to be thinking about was his report, or at least the last paragraph. This job — there were moments when he adored it, when it rushed him onwards as if he were curled in the heart of a wave. And then it would drop him, half-blind with fatigue, and coming home he would fall asleep in the back of a taxi. For the company he felt nothing, neither fondness nor dislike. His father had told him a hundred times of the value of work. The economy had to grow, didn't it? People needed jobs. There was no freedom without free enterprise. He felt tired. He would like to sleep now, leaning back in his chair.

His head cleared. A diamond in the murk. He saw it glimmer. Profit wasn't the real issue, not when the company was scared of store-front locations. A street was open to anyone, anarchic. But a mall was regulated, private, safe. He would recommend that the company identify its outlets only with upscale malls anchored by national tenants. He swivelled to the computer, dropped his hands onto the keyboard, and typed with two fingers, fast:

*The dangerous notion of public access cannot be separated from the marketplace of the street . . .*

And then it was done. He felt the same surge that a poet must, Byron or Keats, on scribbling down the last line. Purified, elevated beyond oneself, alone and free. Masada.

One tap on the keyboard saved the file and two more had it rattling off the printer in the next office. He liked the sound of the printer: like white noise, it dissolved tangles of thoughts. He might be happier walking about with earphones playing that sound, low, like machine guns in a distant war. The printer beeped and he went next door to tear off the paper. He noticed a digital clock on the desk and was surprised to see that it was past eight. Luckily

Claire was understanding, he was amazed at how she put up with him. He bounded down the hall and dropped his report on the girl's desk, her name had vanished again. A good thing he had brought down the car — a person could really drive on the empty Sunday streets.

The elevator doors slid open, splitting his reflection. On King Street the towers had turned into pillars of fire; pages of the *Financial Post* lay scattered across the sidewalk. He hopscotched over the pages, singing under his breath —

*Happy birthday to me,*
*Happy birthday to me,*
*Happy birthday dear Bobby,*
*Happy birthday to me.*

The sun flared behind the houses and went out. Lights came on. The first three stars appeared. Arlene Marks hadn't said a word to anyone for forty minutes. She was hungry, sore, dulled, and furious, and she wanted only to sit down somewhere, away from people. Bobby had kept her waiting once too often, had not shown up, had forgotten a promise. How absurd, the way her heart had pounded when she first came to the apartment door, it had actually hurt her chest. To hell with his birthday. As soon as she was out of here she would phone the airlines and book a plane ticket. For anywhere.

Harold Gross decided never to set foot in his son's apartment again. They were incompetents, the family his son had married into, and Meyer was a jackass. "I've had enough," he announced. "Somebody open that door."

"I think it's locked," said Norman.

"Please," Judy put her hand on her husband's arm, but he shook her off. "We have to think of Claire."

"This *is* getting a little crazy, Mrs. Gross," said Arthur Yates. "Perhaps I can speak to her." He angled his way to the sliding door and tapped with his knuckles. A long minute passed but he just slipped his sunglasses back on. The door slid open several inches. He spoke so quietly that no one could hear him.

From inside, Claire could see Arthur's smile and the others crowded behind. She wanted them to stay outside and wait, for as long as it took. Was that unreasonable? Then she didn't want to be reasonable, she wanted the perfect surprise birthday party.

"Hey Claire," Norman called. "You've got a lynch mob forming out here."

Arthur waved him silent. "I have an idea," he said. "Why don't we change our plans just a tiny bit. We'll come in and sit down, maybe have a bite to eat. We'll just surprise Bobby from in there."

"It won't be as original."

"It'll be very nice."

A pause. Claire's face disappeared and then the door slid open. A scattering of applause broke over the deck as they streamed into the dining room. The table was set with platters of smoked meat, bagels, cole slaw, bottles of wine and Diet Coke. Claire wanted them to have just a taste but they were already digging in with the serving forks and dropping ice cubes into glasses. The first took their plates to the living room and collapsed on the sofa or the arms of chairs to eat. A line-up formed in the hall to the bathroom. The guests found their voices again, laughter travelled around the table, and the food, everyone agreed, was excellent, particularly the pastrami —

The front door jingled. They all heard it; those in the living room could see the doorknob turn. They stopped. The door opened and Bobby, trying to yank his key from the lock, stepped in. "Come on," he muttered, shaking it. He braced the door with his foot. The key came out and, triumphant, he looked up . . . at a lot of people he knew, in his apartment, holding plates.

"Uh, surprise, Bobby," said Norman, holding a speared wedge of tomato.

"Surprise," they said in ragged unison. And started to sing —

*Happy birthday to you,*
*Happy birthday to you . . .*

while Bobby stared at them. He looked from Claire to Lionel to Arlene to his father. He felt an overwhelming desire to yawn. And then annoyance — this was his home, they had no right. The singing stopped and they stood, as if waiting for him to do something. A hard little ball pushed its way up inside his chest, his eyes filmed, he shook with sobs. They loved him, all of them, and they were here to save him. He began to go round the room, from one to another, giving each a hug so forceful that they ached from the strength of his arms.

# The Doctor's House

# ORCHARD

*My* father was a Russian deserter. He was trying to get to France. Tall, with a long, carefully tended moustache and a beautiful bass singing voice.

I learned about him only from Vladislaw the carpenter, who worked in the village near the farm. Vladislaw had one eye, the other had been taken out by a broken bottle in a fight. He wore no patch over the fleshy hole.

When she was sixteen, my mother came into Vladislaw's shop to have a wooden pail mended. My father happened to be in the shop. He still wore his Russian army boots. My mother was just the opposite in build to my father, tiny and plump. No one could understand how she stayed so round when neither she nor her eight brothers and sisters ever had enough to eat. Father called her "my little Moscow sparrow." Two weeks later he disappeared from the village, owing money to all the merchants. And nine months later I was born.

## II

*M*y mother carried me all over Poland, from the German to the Russian border, begging for a few groszy, a heel of bread, a day's work. Of my earliest years I remember roads, open sky, long clouds ribbed like feathers. I remember cold, sputtering fires in the rain, huts with leaking roofs. And hunger.

## III

*W*hen I was five my mother returned to her village. From Vladislaw she heard that Reb Mendelsohn, a Jew, needed a housekeeper. Reb Mendelsohn was the only Jewish farmer in the district. We set off walking and did not reach the farm until sunset.

We came to a white-washed house standing upright on the land. On either side stretched fields, one of ripe wheat, the other grass in which cows grazed. A barn and a chicken coop. And behind the house, rising up a hill, rows of low trees with thick trunks. From their crooked branches hung unripe apples, peaches, pears. My mother held my hand as we walked up to the house. Reb Mendelsohn's wife came to the door. She hired my mother.

Reb Mendelsohn had five children, all boys. Like their father they wore caps and fringed garments and black coats. Reb Mendelsohn had once been the manager of the farm and it was said in the village that he had swindled the owner, a Polish nobleman, by talking him into signing some papers while he was drunk. But later Vladislaw told me that the nobleman squandered his inheritance and to escape prison let the Jew take over the farm and the debts. A few years later the nobleman was cleaning his favourite gun, the one he always took hunting, and blew out his stomach.

## IV

*M*y mother helped Reb Mendelsohn's wife with the household chores, milked the cows and fed the chickens, served the meals, did the washing and sewing, and accompanied her mistress to the village on market days.

I did not play with the Mendelsohn sons. They had their own teacher who lived in the house and who taught them the ways of the Jews. On a hot day when the window was open I could hear their droning voices. What did they learn up there? How to speak the language of demons, to change burning coals into diamonds, to turn a man into a goat?

I was a wild boy and I lived among the trees of the orchard. Each tree began with heavy roots, breaking out of the ground like stiffened elbows. Then the trunk, a hundred years old it was said, rising up to a tangled crown. But I learned to climb those trees, pulling myself up into the branches. From there, I could see smoke winding from the kitchen chimney and peasants in the fields.

Soon I could climb any tree in the orchard, faster than it took to look away and back again. The branches were my cradle and the leaves a curtain that hid me from the world. When my mother came out of the house and called, "Josef, Josef!" I wouldn't move but watched her as she shielded her eyes from the low sun and then turned around and went back inside.

## V

In the late fall the peasants came with their buckets and ladders, and Reb Mendelsohn ran about while they filled the buckets with apples and peaches and pears, late into the night. At sundown fires were lit. In five days the trees were bare and the ground littered with bruised and worm-holed fruit.

And so seven years passed.

## VI

*D*usk. Cold and the sky dark with clouds that rumbled and sparked. My mother, busy in the cellar making preserves, had told me to stay in the kitchen, but I slipped out, drawn by a three-quarter moon that played hide-and-seek in the clouds. Then I ran behind the house, so fast that I was out of breath when I reached the first row of trees. I climbed to the highest branch that could hold my weight and heard it creak under me.

Night came.

An owl circled the chicken coop and beat its wings across the face of the moon.

I heard them before I saw them, coming along the dirt road toward the house. Then the flickering light of torches in a ragged line. They shouted and shook staves in their hands. It seemed to take them a long time to reach the house. A lamp went on in an upstairs window. A horse and rider came galloping down the road and almost trampled some of the marchers, who dispersed, shouted, and swarmed together again. The rider clutched the horse's mane as if he might fall off. When the torch light caught the rider's face, I recognized him as the son of the nobleman who had once owned the farm.

At the front gate the mob stopped and grew quieter, as if not knowing what to do. Then someone threw a stone or a brick and the kitchen window shattered. Laughter. A moment later the door opened and Reb Mendelsohn came out. He walked slowly, his long black coat shining in the moonlight. At the gate he stopped and I guessed that he was speaking. And then the rider on the horse brought his whip down on Reb Mendelsohn's head. The sound of the crack didn't reach me for a long moment. The mob rushed forward and the gate caved in.

A torch landed on the roof. People ran everywhere, the Mendelsohn sons in their night dresses, the villagers with their staves. The horse jumped the broken gate and flew across the yard. A cold rain began to fall. In a second-storey window flames grew, subsided, and grew again. Then the window blew out.

Somewhere in the house my mother screamed.

As I scrambled to get down from the tree I slipped and fell onto my knees. I got up and ran to the house. The sons' teacher lay on the ground as a man kicked him. I slipped on the wet path, reached the kitchen door, and pulled it open. Smoke billowed out. Inside, I could hardly breathe. A kitchen chair was made of fire. My voice choked in my throat. The ceiling throbbed in and out and then, just as it fell upon me, I saw the black Polish sky.

# HOUSE

## VII

The room glowed with dark wood and deep rows of books. There was a spiral step-ladder for reaching the high shelves, a table laden with photographs in silver frames, a carpet of intricate pattern. And in the centre a desk of such enormity, such unimaginable weight, that it wasn't like a desk at all but some monstrous thing that had broken through the earth. It was covered in thick journals and long sheets of paper filled with handwriting.

I was laid out on my back on a velvet divan, a blanket over my legs. I had never seen such a room before or such a house.

A woman came into the room carrying a porcelain bowl. She didn't speak, but I knew what the bowl was for, and when she left I used it, feeling the shame rise in me. Some time later, she came back and took the bowl away.

## VIII

*T*he doctor had a long, creased face, a goatee, and a pince-nez perched on his nose. He wore a striped suit with a vest and heavy shoes. He stood beside me as I stretched out on the divan with my hands wrapped in bandages and my leg encased in plaster.

"How do your hands feel?" he asked. When I didn't answer, he said almost severely, "Don't be shy now."

"They — they sting."

"Can you feel your leg?"

"No. Yes. I think so."

He removed his pince-nez and began to polish it with a handkerchief. Naked, his eyes looked small and weak. "You are a lucky boy, Josef — do you remember what happened?"

"Yes."

"And how you got here — to Warsaw, to this house?"

"I'm not sure."

"A man brought you here in a cart. Reb Mendelsohn was my wife's brother. Your hands are burned, but not severely. Your leg was more badly injured. It was broken in two places, one a compound fracture, and the knee was damaged too. Let's hope for the best. The cast will have to stay on for some weeks. They thought it would be dangerous for you to go to the village. So you'll stay with us until we decide what to do with you. What you need now is rest. Time, Josef, time and patience are what heal."

I wanted to say something. The doctor looked at me. "Yes, Josef. What is it?"

"My mother."

"I'm sorry."

He put his pince-nez back on.

## IX

*I*n the evening, the doctor returned. He called in his daughter and spoke to her in Yiddish. But she answered in Polish.

"I don't want to," she said. "He's one of them, a murderer. I refuse to do anything to help him."

She stood with one hand on her hip and scowled at me. She was much older than me and wore a blue school uniform. Her irises were almost black.

The doctor spoke quietly. "Chava, do not make a difficult situation worse. Do as I say."

He left the room. Chava followed and I heard them on the stairs. Footsteps sounded again and Chava entered, carrying a tray steaming with warm food.

She sat on the edge of the divan. "All right, I'll feed you if I have to. Open your mouth, boy. How do you expect me to get the spoon in?"

She fed me so quickly I hardly had time to swallow. "This is work for a nurse-maid," she said. "I don't know why Papa doesn't let Anya do it. I'm sixteen already, not a child. After the gymnasium I'm going to go to the Sorbonne. You hurry up and get well. My father has important work to do, and so do I. You're in the way."

When she decided that I had eaten enough, she roughly wiped my mouth with a napkin and stood up with the tray in her hands. The skirt of her uniform swayed below her knees.

"What's going to happen to me?"

She narrowed her eyes. "You'll suffer, like everyone else." Then she turned around and closed the door by hooking it with the toe of her shoe.

## X

*O*ne morning Madam Krochmal, the doctor's wife, left the door open. I could see the heavy rail of the bannister and the wallpaper decorated with tiny flowers. A man stepped soundlessly into the doorway and stood there. I knew he must be the grandfather, an old man with a wild beard. He wore no coat but suspenders, while a tangle of fringes dangled from beneath his rumpled shirt. Although he said nothing, his eyes burned fiercely at me, as if to turn me to cinders. I felt myself tremble and closed my eyes. When I opened them again, he was gone.

## XI

*S*ometimes, at night, the doctor sat at his desk and worked. An electric lamp with a green shade cast a circle of light over the books and papers. He came in after I had fallen asleep, but once I woke up and kept still so as not to draw his attention. He wrote slowly and deliberately, without expression, only creasing his brow now and then. But every so often he would put his pen down, touch his long fingers together, and smile dryly, as if he had written something that pleased him.

## XII

*I*n the afternoons I waited for Chava to come home from the gymnasium. I never knew whether she would be friendly or hostile to me, and she kept me in a state of delirious fear.

One night I heard her come in but knew she wasn't alone. A young man's laughter drifted up the stairway. Instead of coming up with my tray, Chava and the young man went into the dining room for their own supper. I strained to hear them moving below.

An hour later, Chava came up with my food. She almost tipped the tray as she whirled into the room, her cheeks flushed. "We've had wine!" she said. "Mendel's telling the most outrageous stories. Oh what a wonderful night I'm having. For the first time in days Papa and

Mamma aren't sitting gloomily at the table. Josef, why haven't you turned on the lamp? Papa's article on reforming medical care for the poor was published in the newspaper today and everybody's talking about it. Tonight some of Papa's friends are coming to congratulate him. Hurry and eat, I've got to help Mamma and Anya in the kitchen."

"Who is Mendel?" I asked, chewing as slowly as I could.

"Oh, Mendel Feltzer. He's already studying medicine at the universit; his marks were so good that he was accepted even with the quota. And he adores me, he tells me that all the time. Of course I don't say anything to encourage him. Hurry up! I have to get out of this stupid uniform."

For a girl who was hurrying, she took an awfully long time to change. On her way down again she came in to pick up the tray. "How do I look?" she asked, holding the fringes of her dress as she turned, the skirt fanning out below her narrow waist. I couldn't speak.

"You're supposed to tell me that I look beautiful."

"You look beautiful."

I couldn't remember ever speaking the word before. Chava picked up the tray and ran out again.

The evening seemed to go on forever. Up the stairs drifted the sound of laughter, of men's voices, of greetings in Yiddish and Polish, of the tinkling of glasses. I couldn't sleep. Finally I heard the last guests close the door behind them. I buried my head in the pillow and closed my eyes. The house became still. Just as I was becoming drowsy,

I felt a hand touch my cheek. Chava stood next to me in the dark. She wore a robe and her hair was tied back.

"Josef, are you awake?"

"Yes."

She sat on the edge of the divan. "You're the only one I can talk to. I hate it here. If I don't get out I'll suffocate, I'll kill myself. Oh God, what am I going to do?"

# ATTIC

## XIII

$\mathcal{I}$ sat on the divan as the doctor snipped at the bandages around my hands and slowly unwound them. Behind him Madam Krochmal stood and watched while behind her Chava bit her lower lip.

"Good, good," the doctor nodded as he turned each hand in his own. "They're fine now, a little scarred, but that is the least important thing. It's not how they look, Josef, but whether they work."

Although I wanted to thank him, I said nothing. Chava stepped forward. "For being such a good patient," she announced, "we reward you with these." And from behind the door she brought out a pair of crutches.

The doctor motioned impatiently with a finger. "Give

them to me, please, Chava." She demurred, but when he looked at her over the top of his lenses, she handed them to him. "Now Josef," he said, "you must go slowly and carefully at first. Try not to put weight on the cast. Chava will show you the proper way to use them."

And they were mine. I was no longer a prisoner in the doctor's study. The crutches were not new but well worn, the hand-rests smoothed by countless palms. I pulled myself up from the divan and tucked them under my arms, the way I'd seen one of the village beggars do, who had a stump for a leg. But a moment later I tipped forward and the doctor caught me around the shoulders.

"You're quite an athlete, boy," Chava laughed.

"Chava, do not call Josef 'boy.' He isn't a servant."

"Yes, Papa."

"I must get to the hospital. But first I wish to reclaim my study. Chava, you are to move Josef upstairs to the attic room with you."

"Are you joking?"

"There's an extra bed up there and more than enough room."

Chava actually stamped her foot on the carpet. "But Papa, this is too much! I can't sleep in the same room as — as some orphan."

"I don't have time to be angry with you, Chava. You know the house is cramped because of my need for a surgery and a study. The attic is easy to divide — just hang up some sort of curtain. Josef's still a child, he's quite harmless. These days many people sleep two or three to a bed and some families are glad to have a cellar. When are you going to learn that the world was not constructed solely for your pleasure? The discussion is over. I'll see you all at dinner."

"I think I'm going to die," Chava said.

The ladder to the attic was narrow and steep, but Chava refused to help me. I thought I would fall backwards from dizziness before I emerged through the trap door and into the attic.

The ceiling sloped down towards one long side of the room and two windows jutted out like boxes. In the centre was an iron stove, the chimney rising through the ceiling. Chava had a brass bedstead, a dresser and bureau, a desk and chair, and a small bookshelf. Hand-coloured engravings of theatrical scenes were tacked to the wooden braces on the walls.

At the other end was an iron bedstead that sagged beneath me when I sat down. Chava rummaged around in a drawer, then strung a rope across the room's width and draped an old blanket over it. The blanket hung above the floor and didn't reach the walls, but it made two separate spaces of the room. Then she pushed the blanket aside and strode up to me.

"I want you to understand that this is my room and you are a temporary guest brought here by some unfair accident of fate."

"I'm sorry. I won't be any trouble to you."

"You are trouble to me already, merely by existing. Can't you see that I'm a sensitive person? One day I'm going to be an artist or perhaps an actress. It's only in this room that I can really express my soul, where I can dream. How can I express my soul with you around? How can

I recite poetry or rehearse my part for the next play of the theatre group? And my friends and I formed a literary club, we read books that our teachers don't approve of, Zola and Ibsen. So you see, there's no room for you here."

Chava stood with her arms at her waist and blew out a little sound of impatience from between her lips. She looked away, toward the ceiling, as if she was already thinking deeply about something else.

"Chava," I said. It was the first time I had spoken her name. "Will you teach me to read?"

## XIV

*T*he life of the house was strange and bewildering. Every moment meant some new crisis, some new rush of activity. Chava flung herself about the house, crying that she was late for this or that, couldn't find a pair of stockings, would never memorize her lines in time, had some unsolvable mathematical problem to complete. Yet it was the doctor who had the most to do, working quietly and without fuss. Up first in the morning, he was at his desk as the sun rose over the chimneys and steeples that could be seen in the distance from his window. One morning he caught me watching him from the doorway. He asked me in and explained that he was writing a paper called "Poverty-Related Deaths in the Jewish District of Warsaw." He said, "You can tell a lot about a people by how they die." Then he gave me one of the hard candies that he kept in his pockets for young patients.

Most mornings the doctor did not stay for breakfast but left to make his house calls on the way to the hospital, carrying a scuffed leather bag. Chava could hardly sit down as she ate, jumping up to fetch some school book or assignment that she had forgotten. After she left, the house became quiet.


## XV


When the grandfather moved about the rooms, I imagined a dark mist encircling his body. Every morning and afternoon he visited a place of worship that Chava said was no more than a room in an apartment off Nalewki Street. Through a window I would see him shuffling down the road with his hat back on his head and his coat-tails swaying. He never looked to the left or right but kept his eyes on the ground.

Returning, he always went straight down to the cellar. The cellar door was in the main hall, painted brown instead of varnished like the others, and what he did down there was a mystery to me. One night I dreamed he was chasing me through a field of wheat. His hands and feet had grown claws, his black coat was a mile long, his beard entangled me like a vine. When I awoke the bed was wet and acrid-smelling. Chava smelled it too and made a terrible row, demanding that I be removed from the attic. But by the evening she had forgotten about it.

## XVI

The students began to arrive shortly after dinner, hanging about the courtyard behind the house while the doctor attended to the patients who came in the evening, when he gave aid without fee. After the last patient left, Chava let the students into the front vestibule, and they removed their hats as they filed up the stairway and crowded into the surgery, which was connected by a doorway to the doctor's study.

Chava had already told me that the doctor had taught at the university for almost twenty years, until he had suddenly been dismissed. Instead of protesting he merely devoted more time to the hospital and his private practice, but shortly afterwards a delegation of Jewish students approached him. They complained of attempts to keep them out of the classrooms and laboratories. Several had been attacked upon leaving the library after dark. They asked the doctor whether he would conduct an informal class to help the students surmount these discriminations.

I watched the students from the doorway, Mendel Feltzer among them. The doctor stood beside a human skeleton that hung from a metal stand. "Good evening, gentlemen," he said. "I see we have quite a good turnout tonight. Am I correct in my suspicion that examinations are fast approaching?" The students laughed. "This evening we shall continue our review of the degenerative diseases of the spinal column. Let us begin."

## XVII

$\mathcal{F}$lakes of snow alighted on the attic window, melted, and ran down the glass. I could barely see the street below as I sat on the sill, half twisted towards the window, my cast pointed at the warm stove.

"I'll never get this right," Chava groaned. She was sprawled on her bed, writing in a notebook.

"What are you doing?" I asked.

"I'm trying to rewrite my skit for the Zionist theatre night. The director says it isn't politically accurate. Even though it's a love story! You see" — she sat up, tucking one leg under herself — "in my skit a man and a woman fall madly in love. Only, they can't marry because the woman has planned to go to Paris to become a ballerina while the man refuses to leave Warsaw, where his mother is dying. I can't decide how to end it — for art, romance, or family. The director wants me to make the man a labourer who wishes to smuggle them to Palestine. But I can't let my poor woman give up her dream of being a dancer just to dig irrigation ditches in the desert! I have to write what I feel. But what do I really feel? I've had no experience in love or anything else."

She sighed dramatically and fell back onto her pillow.

I said, "Don't you love Mendel Feltzer?"

She laughed. "Josef, you ask funny questions. Every day Mendel asks me to marry him. He's very sweet but to him I'm perfect and can do no wrong. How could I love a man like that? Besides, Mendel is like Papa, dedicated to his boring medicine. I think about leaving Warsaw every day."

She got up from the bed and came over to the window. "So winter is finally here," she said and sat down beside me. "Just think, right now people all over the world are looking out of windows. In Vienna, Paris, America, even India. Sometimes I imagine that I can see through the eyes of another person somewhere else in the world, maybe even in another time. And that person can see through mine, so that in my head I have to explain just what happens in this building, or who lives on that street. I might as well imagine, because there's no chance of my going anywhere. Papa would never think of leaving. Over the last ten months he's aged years. So many sick people, so many students asking for his help. He doesn't think twice about treating someone who can't pay. That's all very well, but Mamma has to pay the bills. Just the other day the butcher came to the door demanding money. Poor Mamma was so embarrassed, she had to give him three silver spoons just to make him stop shouting.

"Last night I dreamed that I was looking down from this window at hundreds of people. They surrounded the house, Papa's patients, sores on their bodies, missing limbs, all moaning and weeping, crying for Papa to save them. They pressed against the walls of the house so hard that it trembled. I started screaming at them to go away and then I woke up. It was still dark, my heart was beating. Josef, I'm scared of those people."

## XVIII

$O$ne night during dinner the family held a meeting. I stood behind the glass doors etched with a geometric pattern that separated the dining room from the sitting room. While they spoke Anya brought the dishes in from the kitchen. The doctor asked the family what they ought to do with me. He had already made enquiries in the village where I was born, but my mother's relatives refused to take me in. The only other place was the orphanage.

Madam Krochmal said, "Perhaps he'd be safer there than in our house. Look what's happening in Germany."

Chava just stared at a porcelain bowl on the table, as if she were incapable of speaking. Finally she said, "He's always watching me. He thinks I don't know it, but I do."

"So then it's decided?" the doctor asked.

Madam Krochmal and Chava looked down at the table. They both started when the grandfather clanged his fork down onto his plate. He wiped at his beard. He said, "Let the boy stay awhile yet." And picked up his fork again.

## XIX

$\mathcal{A}$s I lay on the examining table in the surgery, the doctor cut open the cast with a big pair of scissors. He pulled apart the two halves like the shell of a nut. My leg lay limply on the table, red and withered.

"Try to stand," the doctor said, helping me down. He caught me as I fell. But he made me try again and this time I could put some weight on it while he gripped my arm.

For several days I still needed the crutches to move about, but soon I could walk on my own again. But the leg would never be right. The knee had been damaged and would hardly bend. I now walked with a step swing, step swing motion.

## XX

$\mathcal{T}$he letters of the alphabet looked all the same to me, the rules too complicated to remember. I blushed as I stumbled over the simplest words while Chava called me idiot, simpleton, imbecile. Several times a lesson she announced that it was no use, she was giving up in despair. Then she would become patient and gentle as we started again. Sitting next to me, her hair brushing my face, she urged me on with a mixture of taunts and encouragements. After several weeks she even became caught up in my progress, so determined for me to improve that she would come home early from her meetings and rehearsals to give us more time. While she was away at school, I copied out row after row of letters, clutching the pencil near its tip. Chava said my letters looked like squashed beetles.

## XXI

*I* tried to open the cellar door without making a sound, but it made a long and dreary creak. The stairs descended between brick walls into the ground and a light from below spilled onto the bottom steps. My hands pressed against the cold brick and my footsteps sounded hollow on the stone.

At the bottom was a beam so low I had to stoop. The smell was dense, moist, and heavy. I heard paper rustling, a phlegmy cough, but the small space was so crowded I couldn't see where the sounds came from. Scarred wooden tables were burdened with strange equipment, while the shelves along the walls held iron tools and rolls of leather. And books lay everywhere, giant tomes piled on the floor and little volumes, no bigger than my palm, lined in rows.

The grandfather was hunched over a table near the back with a lamp glowing beside him. An iron pot stood on the table, blackened with soot from the flame underneath. He stuck a round-headed brush into the pot, mixed it about, and then forcefully dabbed the brush against the spine of a large, coverless book held in a vice.

The grandfather looked at me with one eye but continued to work the glue into the spine. I breathed a little easier and looked about at the books in various states of repair. Some had bare boards for covers, others had been reduced to mere piles of sheets. In one corner stood a great iron press with a wheel to screw down, a stack of books caught in its jaws. And on a square table a book with a shining leather cover rested beside a stand of wooden-handled tools. I picked up one and examined the gouged-out brass end. Pressing it against my palm left the impression of a Hebrew letter.

When I picked up a knife to see how sharp it was, the grandfather came over and took it out of my hand. He led me to a table and sat me down on a bench. He didn't speak but pulled a pile of sheets from a drawer and lay them before me. He picked up a white stick, flat and with one rounded and one pointed end, just large enough to fit in the hand. Pulling a sheet forward, he leaned over me and folded it in half, running the edge of the stick along the fold to make the crease. He put the sheet aside, pulled another forward, and lay the stick in my hand.

The stick was smooth to the touch and slightly porous, and I could tell that it was made of bone. I looked up questioningly at him, but he merely stared severely back. So I tried to fold the sheet as he had, only it bent in the wrong place. He put his hands over mine to guide them. We pressed the stick over the crease together. The next one I managed by myself, and when I looked over my shoulder, he raised one bushy eyebrow and went back to his own bench.

I drew another sheet. Soon the stick felt good in my hand and the folds became neater. I worked with concentration while the grandfather worked at his own table, and the only sound was of paper and hands.

## XXII

"A pleasure to see you, Sholem," said a red-faced man as he held his hand out to the doctor. "How I look forward to these gatherings of yours. But who's that lurking in the parlour? Syrkin, it's you, the devil himself. I've got a word to say about that last column of yours. It isn't as easy as that to dismiss the art theatre."

So Franz Edelstadt, the playwright, entered Doctor Krochmal's house and after him came others. These literary evenings were invasions from a world outside that baffled and excited me. I watched from the top of the stairs as the guests gave their coats and hats to Anya and drifted noisily into the parlour. Their voices grew steadily, along with the clinking of cups and saucers.

Just as it seemed that everyone had arrived and the hall was empty, a knock sounded on the door. The doctor ushered in a young man in a threadbare overcoat. He had downcast eyes and a pinched mouth. Doctor Krochmal greeted him by his name, Fagenbaum, and drew him towards the parlour. "I almost didn't hear you come in," the doctor said. "It's a good thing you've arrived, we old men need to rub shoulders with some young blood. Have you brought some poems to read tonight?"

"No, I . . . well, yes."

"Splendid. Come right in, don't be frightened, everyone's here."

I slid down the stairs with my stiff leg straight and slipped into the dining room, from where I could view the gathering through the glass doors. Anya had moved to the samovar, where she poured cups of tea, which Madam Krochmal herself passed on to the guests, while Chava handed out plates of honey cake. I knew from Chava that some of these writers had run away from their homes to seek a modern education, to learn about art and science. But to me, even in their western suits, smoking cigarettes, they looked like Jews. It was the way they nodded from the waist and stroked their short beards or bare chins. They spoke and argued all at the same time. In one corner Shatzky, a socialist, shook his finger at a poet named Epstein who, Chava had told me, was an "aesthete." In another the publisher Ornitz listened sceptically to a proposal from a novelist named Gutkind, who made his living translating French romances into Yiddish. All the while Doctor Krochmal moved from one conversation to another, listening, shaking his head, a tall figure leaning over the others.

Ravnitsky, the essayist, was saying, "If we ever want to have a respected literature, one that will stand up in Paris or London, we must forgo the past and become truly modern. Our novelists are a hundred years out of date, trapped in the confines of bourgeois Romanticism. And those who aren't are burdened by our traditions and our faith. They hang about our necks like dead children."

His words caused a storm of protest, from a dozen points of view. In the midst of the arguments a knock came from the front door, although at first no one seemed to hear it. Finally Madam Krochmal left the room and returned with a small man, who held her arm. He had a fringe of straw-white hair on his otherwise bald head, and his cheeks were red from the cold.

Doctor Krochmal called out, "Good evening, welcome, Eliezer Zametkin," and shook his hand. "What a pleasure to have you join us."

"Sholem, how good to see you. To see all of you. I wish I could come more often, but these days I stay in a good deal. I haven't so many years left to finish my work, although, of course, there are those who think I've written too many books already!"

His laugh came out as a wheeze. The others moved forward to shake his hand. Chava had told me about Eliezer Zametkin, but I found it hard to match this simple-looking man with the way she had spoken. He was over seventy now, but as a young man he had travelled to the smallest villages, talking to people and recording their stories, thus gathering the material for his writings.

Anya and Madam Krochmal could barely keep up with the demand for fresh cups of tea. The coal fire blazed in the hearth and the room became stifling, but the conversation did not slacken. At one point a collection was taken up for a writer named Ettinger whose health had become bad and who was about to be evicted from his room on Leszno Street.

The young poet, Fagenbaum, stood quietly most of the evening but finally ventured to ask Eliezer Zametkin a question. "Please, if you would," he stumbled, "how did you come to write your story 'Death and His Lover?' It is as timeless as a folk tale, yet modern at the same time. I hardly understand how it works, only that it leaves an ache in my heart."

Eliezer Zametkin smiled. "I heard that story in a tiny prayer house outside of Lemberg. Told by a man with such feeling, such sweetness of tone that I could only capture a part of that voice in my own. Of course I altered it: the perspective is different, one character added and another taken out. And the ending, well that adds something of my own. But it's from that prayer house that the voice came. It's where all our inspiration comes, whether we are able to pray or not."

## XXIII

*W*inter finally gave in to spring. Every afternoon, when the rest of the family was out, I went down to the cellar to help the grandfather. I scraped away old glue on spines, sat at the sewing frame and slipped needle and thread through sections of leaves, cut boards with a heavy knife. Before dinner Chava gave me my lessons. She was kinder now, tousled my hair, told me everything that happened to her. Doctor Krochmal began arriving home later from the hospital, and there were always patients waiting on the bench in the surgery, coughing into their handkerchiefs or holding infants in their laps. I felt strangely angry at these ragged people for disrupting the household. Yet I almost forgot that there had been any life before this one. I dreamed that I would live in this house forever.

# THE AMERICAN

## XXIV

"*I* got a letter today," Madam Krochmal said as we settled down around the dinner table. I now ate with the rest of the family instead of in the kitchen. "It's from my sister Bessie in New York City."

"Let me read it aloud!" Chava cried.

"No, I think I'll read it myself." She could not suppress a grin as she pulled the letter from the pocket of her dress. It was written in Yiddish, which I could now understand and even speak, although neither Chava nor anyone else had taught me.

"'My dearest sister, I have some very exciting news for you. First I report that Ephraim managed to get that large government contract for uniforms that I wrote you about, so the factory will be humming right through until fall. But the real news is about our son Israel. As you know, Israel is already twenty-three but has had some trouble settling down to a serious adult life. This is the way all young men are in America. But he is very intelligent, handsome, and speaks like a prince. That he should use such gifts for good purposes only!

"'Israel is now old enough to take up his full position in the business. But still he is restless and resists his responsibilities. He says the world is a big place and he has seen only one small part of it. Imagine, Leah, he desires to travel! In our day a Jew would be born in Vitebsk, live all his days in Vitebsk, and die in Vitebsk. Naturally Ephraim and I have exchanged a few hot words over this, but in the end we decided that if a little travel will help Israel settle down, then it's worth it. Only we would not let him go just anywhere. We told Israel, go and visit your relatives in Warsaw who you have never met.

"'Yes, it's true! Our Israel is coming to spend the summer with you. I myself often grow homesick for the old sights, in spite of how blessed our lives have been here. To visit my dear sister, our brothers, and the graves of our parents! I am too old now, but at least I can send my son.

"'In just two days Israel will board a ship to Hamburg, and then take a train to Warsaw. I will wire you his arrival time. Please meet him at the station, as he speaks no Polish and his Yiddish is full of American words. Leah, keep an eye on my eldest son. He is a good boy but spirited. With him I send you my love. Bessie.'"

There was not a sound in the room. Chava stared at her mother in a way that frightened me, as if she were asleep though her eyes were open. "Is it true?" she frowned. "My cousin is coming from America. All the way across the ocean. But why would he come here?"

"I must admit it's extraordinary," said the doctor. "He's certainly welcome in our house. I look forward to talking with this young man — there are many questions about America that I'd like to ask."

"When I think how much there is to do before his arrival!" Madam Krochmal said. "After all, his parents have done very well for themselves. I'm sure they've given him the best of everything. But where will he sleep?"

Chava got up from her chair and stood by the table. "I don't see why he's coming at all, when we're so busy just now. He'll disrupt everything."

"Don't be silly," Madam Krochmal said. "We'll have to buy you a new dress. And as for you," she said to her father-in-law, "you must have a new coat whether you want one or not. Look at the threads hanging from that old rag."

The grandfather didn't even look up.

## XXV

"*W*e lived on the seventh floor on Delancey Street. Eight people shared our apartment, and six families used one toilet at the end of the hall. I was too young to remember much, but I remember how scared I was sleeping on the floor. At night the bugs crawled over you. No matter how much Mamma cleaned she couldn't get rid of them."

Israel had been given my chair at the dinner table across from Chava and I had been moved down. Madam Krochmal served a roasted chicken, the biggest I'd ever seen, and to her delight Israel cried with pleasure at every new dish Anya brought in from the kitchen.

"We lived on Delancey until my father was promoted to head tailor in the coat department," Israel said. "Then we moved into our own apartment on Orchard Street. Mamma too did piecework. It took ten years before he could start up his own business. From two machines to a whole floor, and from a floor to a factory. Now we have a big house in Brooklyn, our own car, and every summer Mamma spends three weeks in the Catskill mountains with my sisters."

"How wonderful," Madam Krochmal said. "We read about such stories in the newspapers. Tell me, Israel, do you remember anything at all about Poland?"

"No, I was too young. As far as I'm concerned I'm one hundred percent American."

Doctor Krochmal said, "Did you see anything disturbing on the train from Hamburg, any signs? Did you have any trouble?"

"Please, Sholem, let's not talk about such things tonight. This is a celebration."

"Have you been to the Broadway theatres?" Chava asked.

"More times than I can count."

The doctor said, "I have read that crowding in the Lower East Side is not as bad as a decade ago. This must have a positive effect on the rate of illness."

"If I lived in America," Chava said, "I would go to the theatre every night. And I'm sure I could go to university, couldn't I, Israel?"

"Questions, questions! What do you expect from the boy?" Madam Krochmal said. "Give him a chance to breathe."

"I really don't mind."

Doctor Krochmal pulled his watch from his pocket. "Excuse our enthusiasm, Israel. In any case, the time has slipped by and I must attend to my patients."

"Israel has a wristwatch," Chava said. "I noticed it at the station."

"Everybody in America has one," he smiled. "It's more practical."

"I'll come and help you, Papa," Chava said.

"No, stay and entertain your cousin. You've helped me every night this week."

"Wait," Israel said, jumping up from his chair. "Nobody move just for a moment. I'll be right back. Chava, turn on all the lights."

He sprinted from the room. Chava laughed as she turned on the lamps, making the room bright.

"What is he up to?" the doctor asked.

Then Israel was back, holding a black metal box to his eye as he turned a small crank. "Smile!" he cried. "Do something!"

"What is it?" Madam Krochmal sounded frightened.

"It's a camera, a moving-picture camera. I bought it just before leaving."

"That's fantastic," said Doctor Krochmal. "Israel will be able to show moving pictures of us back in America."

"Point it at me!" Chava laughed. "Point it at me! Look, I'm dancing for the moving-picture camera!"

## XXVI

*M*adam Krochmal sat in a big armchair with her sewing in her lap. In her new white dress, Chava played the "Moonlight" Sonata while Israel leaned on the piano and gazed at her pale neck. His eyes had a half-closed and dreamy look. A forelock of hair almost touched his eyelashes.

When Chava lingered on the last chord, he clapped his hands. "Wonderful, cousin. With such talent you'd be a welcome guest in the best homes in New York. None of their daughters play as well. In comparison, they're vulgar."

"I really think I should go help Papa," Chava said without looking away from the sheet music. "Otherwise he'll be in the surgery all night."

"Let me play you some new American songs. Did you ever hear of Irving Berlin?"

Chava got up carefully so as not to crease her dress.

XXVII

*M*adam Krochmal decided that it would be most proper if Israel slept in the attic while Chava made the divan in the study her bed. He climbed the stairs after me and pulled himself up through the trap door.

"I'm beat," he said, lying on his back on Chava's bed. "What a city! I feel as if I've gone back in time a hundred years. I've got an idea, Josef. How about you doing me a favour and unpacking my clothes? Make sure you hang the trousers up."

When I opened the trunk, it smelled of crushed flowers. "Be careful with those ties, they're silk," he called. "So this is where cousin Chava slept. Lucky you, not that you'd appreciate it. Hey, watch what you're doing," he said and, springing up from the bed, pushed me aside. He lifted a pile of shirts — pale blue, yellow, I'd never seen such colours. Underneath were nestled two pistols. They had ivory grips and long, elaborately engraved barrels.

"Aren't they beauties?" Israel said as he lifted one in his hands. He said their name in English — Colt Peacemakers — and made me pronounce the words, laughing when they came out wrong. Then he put them in an old armoire, under some bed linen.

We undressed for bed. Israel was slender and almost hairless, his skin golden. He looked at me and laughed.

"What's so funny?" I asked.

"You. Imagine them telling people that you're a distant relative. When you're not even circumcised! Look at that prick, it's disgusting. No one would believe you're a member of the family."

"We have to pretend, it's the rule."

"And what if I broke the rule? Not that there's anyone to tell, even if I wanted to. Get into bed, Josef. I'm turning out the light."

## XXVIII

On Saturday the family returned from the Tlomackie Synagogue in high spirits. "What an impression Israel made," Madam Krochmal glowed. "Everyone wanted to speak to him. I never received so many invitations to tea in my life."

"But did they have to ask such stupid questions?" Chava said. "As if Israel were a personal acquaintance of President Roosevelt."

"Don't exaggerate, Chava," Doctor Krochmal said. "And you weren't such an expert on America before you started peppering Israel with questions."

"Everyone was very kind," said Israel.

## XXIX

"*A* girl like you isn't meant to be so serious, nor to be forced into so many responsibilities."

"I'm not forced. It's my choice."

"You only convince yourself of that. I'll tell you what is happening. You're becoming old before your time."

"And America is better? I know what goes on. All you care about there is money."

"Is that so wrong? Money may be nothing in itself, but it brings freedom."

"Ah, you're impossible to talk to. Only in America do people hold such naive ideas."

"Chava, even though I haven't known you very long, I can tell that you're not an ordinary girl. Who are you helping if your talents are stifled? If a rose doesn't get rain it withers."

"That's trite. I'm no flower. Let's change the subject. Tomorrow I'm going to show you the Saxon Garden. It's so beautiful this time of year, filled with real flowers. Everywhere nannies are pushing carriages and there's even an orchestra. Israel, I'm glad you've come. I do feel that things are changing. Something special is going to happen."

## XXX

$\mathcal{D}$octor Krochmal and his wife had an argument when Israel and Chava were out. Their raised voices could be heard through the house. For some reason that she refused to explain, Madam Krochmal's attitude to her nephew had altered. She wanted her husband to forbid Chava from going about the streets, to restaurants and movie houses, with Israel.

"But why shouldn't they go out?" the doctor asked. "Fine weather draws young people out of doors. Sometimes I wonder what it's doing to Chava, working next to me every night, seeing so much suffering. It's good for her to forget for a short while."

"God forgive me, Israel may be my sister's son, but he's not honest with us."

"Naturally young people have their secrets. Why should Israel and Chava want to be around old people like us? Leah, let them be."

"That's all very well, but what will be the result? It's not good for her to build up expectations."

"Of what kind? Israel's here for just a little while. In fact I'm going to tell him that he should leave as soon as possible. Who knows when even an American passport won't get a person across the border? In the meantime we should let Chava have some pleasure for a few more days. Don't you trust our daughter?"

"Sholem, after all these years as a doctor you still understand nothing about people."

## XXXI

*A*fter the last patient of the evening had gone, Doctor Krochmal worked at his desk in the study, his long face lit by the lamp with the green shade. I knocked on the open door and when he answered I stepped inside.

The doctor appeared mildly surprised to see me, as it was several hours after the time I went to bed. I tried to speak, but my throat seemed to swell up.

"Did you have a bad dream, Josef? It'll be all right, go back to sleep."

"Doctor." My voice came out as a whisper. "I want to be like you."

He smiled. "Like me? A doctor? Perhaps some day, after a good deal of hard work and study."

"No, I mean like you and other men. Jews. I want to be like you here."

I pointed shamefacedly to what I meant. The doctor looked astonished. "You want to be circumcised?"

"Yes, I want to be circumcised like a Jew."

"I just don't know. That is, if I have any authority to do such a thing. And you're not a baby — it would hurt afterward."

"Please."

"I admit that it's better, hygienically, that is. I might even recommend it under certain circumstances. Still, I had better talk to my wife about this. What a strange request, Josef. Let me think about it."

I climbed up to the attic and buried myself under the

blankets. Israel was not yet home; he had begun going out in the evenings by himself and not returning until early morning. For a long time I lay shivering in the dark.

## XXXII

*A* week later Doctor Krochmal performed the surgery, assisted by two medical students. The procedure went smoothly — merely the removal of a piece of skin — but afterwards the wound wouldn't close and the bandage had to be replaced frequently. In the middle of the night I woke up, the bed full of blood. After three days the bleeding stopped. Only a dull ache remained.

## XXXIII

*W*hile I was convalescing, Israel stumbled up the ladder to the attic, singing in English under his breath. He smelled of vodka. It took him several tries to unbutton his shirt. He lay down on his bed in his underpants, laughed, and then choked for a moment.

"You don't understand, Josef," he said. "New York isn't like this mud hole. In New York there's plenty of opportunity for a man who's got a head on his shoulders.

You understand me? My father, he worked like a slave for twenty years, twelve hours a day. Even now he doesn't let up. But that's not for me, I'll tell you that. And I was doing very well for myself too. All right, I was only dealing in small merchandise — Indian rugs, radios, that sort of thing. But it was profitable work. I was good at it, people liked me. You want to know why I'm here? One day a man comes to me, he says that a shipment of first-class beaver coats is coming into the city. And this man just happens to know that a hundred of these coats are somehow going to get misplaced when the train stops on the other side of the Hudson River. Would I like to be the one to find them? It's a big step for me, but an opportunity like this doesn't come around the corner every day. The only hitch is that I've got to pay half the money up front. So I go to a couple of brothers I'd heard about who work out of a restaurant on Fifty-Second Street. They have a table at the back permanently on reserve for them, and their own telephone too. Sure, they're delighted to help a young Rockefeller find his feet. Two nights later I wait with a van behind the loading dock of the station in New Jersey. Only, the train doesn't stop, the furs keep right on going."

Israel laughed as he fumbled with a cigarette. "I go looking all over for the man who told me about them, in every bar on the East Side, but he's vanished. Two days later a couple of messengers from the brothers come looking for me. I try to explain and they leave me bent over in an alley, with a promise of worse to come if I don't get them their money. What can I do but humiliate myself and crawl to my father? But all his money is tied up in inventory for army uniforms, every last nickel, and he won't start getting paid for another three months. He's just got enough money for a boat ticket and two days later I'm leaning over a rail waving to the Statue of Liberty."

He took a long drag on his cigarette, making the end glow in the darkness.

"I wonder what time it is in New York?" he sighed. "This little exile of mine would be unbearable if it weren't for Chava. She's a pearl, my cousin. The truth is I'm becoming too attached to her."

# WAR

## XXXIV

From the attic, Israel, Chava, and I watched the marchers fill the streets below. The words they chanted sounded like a terrible roar. The sun flashed on the rims of eyeglasses, on policemen's badges, on horses' bridles.

"If only I could go down and join them," Chava said. "Papa doesn't have the right to forbid me."

"Chava," Israel said, "I want to save you from this. There's still time to get out of here. Let me take you to America. My father has connections in the government. But we have to act right away."

"How can you even ask me at this moment? I don't know anything. I only know that my father's own students are down there."

"We should stay out of it."

"You stay out of it then."

"Chava, this isn't real, it's just a bad dream. And you can wake up whenever you want."

"Maybe you're the one living in a dream, not I. Maybe America is just a dream. Why do I just stand here? I ought to be doing something. Before you came, Israel, I never hesitated like this. I'm beginning to hate you."


## XXXV


*S*ummer was over. The orderly running of the house had disintegrated. The telephone rang incessantly as one crisis after another took the doctor out at any hour. One morning Madam Krochmal discovered that Anya had fled back to her family in the country. She had to go into the streets by herself to find enough food for the household. The grandfather stayed in his room and prayed.

Israel booked his passage, cancelled the ticket, and then booked it again. "This is crazy," he said, rocking on the edge of his bed. "I should have left weeks ago. I don't know what's come over me."

## XXXVI

One night I could not sleep. From the sky came rumblings and flashes of light. Israel's bed was empty. I put on my clothes and climbed down the ladder. The house was filled with a translucent green darkness as I wandered from room to room as if I would never see it again.

I heard a noise from the surgery. The door was open and I stood in the doorway. Israel and Chava were on the surgery bed. They were naked. Israel was above her, arching his slender back, his face in a grimace. Chava had her fingers tangled in his hair. I could see the dark line of her tense body. She made a sound that was unbearable to hear. But I stood there, I stood there.

## XXXVII

Before morning, the war started. I stood at the attic window and watched the sky become bright with explosions. I knew that bridges were collapsing, the glass roofs of railway stations falling in. A fog drifted low in the air.

## XXXVIII

*W*hen the aeroplanes reached Warsaw, I recognized them from the newspaper illustrations I had studied — Heinkel and Dornier bombers, accompanied by Messerschmitt 109s. It was as if day had turned suddenly to night. The noise was deafening, and the house shook. A fine powder fell into my hair and eyes.

Everyone began shouting and running about. Madam Krochmal cried, "My father's gone crazy, he's gone crazy!" She was leaning out the kitchen window and looking up. I could see her from the attic window, and I opened it and pulled myself half into the air. On the roof above was the grandfather. He had piled the largest books into a kind of tower and had managed to climb on top of them. At every explosion I could see him wave his hands and shout into the sky. He was cursing God.

## XXXIX

*I*n the surgery Doctor Krochmal packed his medical bag. He filled it methodically with bandages and medicines before snapping it shut.

"What are you doing?" Chava cried as she watched him. The doctor smiled sadly at his daughter and kissed her on the forehead. "I'm going to my patients," he said. Then he walked past us.

"Where are the Americans, where are the Americans?" shouted Israel as he rushed down the hall, pushing past the doctor. He held up his two pistols in the air as he ran down the stairway and out the door to the street.

Chava and I followed the doctor after him. People were running everywhere, clasping children or suitcases. A riderless horse galloped by. From above came a screaming, and we looked up to see an aeroplane filling the sky above us. I recognized it as a Messerschmitt fighter even as it roared down toward the street.

Doctor Krochmal pulled us into the doorway of the house. The people scattered, except for Israel, who stood in the middle of the street firing his Colt Peacemakers at the Messerschmitt. The noise of the aeroplane was terrible, its ugly snout grew huge, and I buried my face in the doctor's overcoat.

When I opened my eyes again I saw that the Messerschmitt had landed. Smoke rose from the engine, and the propeller still turned. Its wings almost touched the houses on either side.

Israel was underneath the wheel. He had been crushed. His eyes were open, and his beautiful tie flapped in the wind. Chava sobbed. Doctor Krochmal gently let us go and walked over to Israel. He kneeled down to measure Israel's pulse and then continued past the aeroplane, holding his bag stiffly at his side. I saw him disappear behind a burning house.

"Come with me," I said, and grabbed Chava's hand.

"Josef, what are you doing?"

I didn't answer but pulled her into the street. As we stepped over the rubble, I found a painter's ladder and carried it to the side of the aeroplane. It was hard to climb the ladder with my bad leg, and I had to pull with all my strength to open the cockpit.

Inside, the pilot sat upright. A single bullet had entered his forehead. I unbuckled his straps and hauled him out, letting him fall to the ground.

Chava shrieked. I almost fell down the ladder in my hurry, pushing her up ahead of me again. She obeyed silently, climbing inside first for me to sit, cramped, on her lap. Closing the cockpit from inside was easier.

"We can't go away, we can't," Chava said.

"I'm sure I can fly an aeroplane," I said. "It's just like climbing a tree."

The engine was still humming. As I pulled on the throttle, it began to roar and the Messerschmitt to roll down the street faster and faster, the needles on the dials spinning round. And then, as I eased the stick towards me, the Messerschmitt lifted into the air.

## XL

We rose and banked, over the Royal Castle, the marketplace of the Old Town, the river. The city fell far, far behind us.

"Where are you taking us?" Chava asked. "To America?"

"No, not to America," I said.

"Then where?"

"North," I said.

"North," she repeated.

I knew that it would be wild and cold there. I knew that nobody would ever find us.